GHOST GIRLS AND RABBITS

GHOST GIRLS AND RABBITS

Cassondra Windwalker

POLYMATH
— PRESS —

Aurora, CO

Ghost Girls and Rabbits by Cassondra Windwalker

This book is a work of fiction. All incidents, events, characters, names, business, places, and other entities depicted are either fictitious or are used fictitiously.

Copyright © 2025 by Cassondra Windwalker
Cover art: Spraycasso
Author photograph: Cassondra Windwalker
Design and layout: Robert Lewis

All rights reserved. No portion of this book may be reproduced in any form without written permission from the publisher or copyright holder.

Published by Polymath Press, a trade name of Polymath Enterprises, LLC. Please direct all inquiries to Polymath Press, P. O. Box 461870, Aurora, CO 80046-1870, online at www.polymathpress.com, or via email to editor@polymathpress.com.

First edition

ISBN (paperback): 978-1-961827-08-0
ISBN (eBook): 978-1-961827-09-7
Library of Congress Control Number: 2025934794

Other Works by Cassondra Windwalker

Humantale (November 2024)

What Hides In the Cupboards (January 2024)

Love Like A Cephalopod (February 2023)

Hold My Place (January 2022)

The Bench (July 2021)

tide tables and tea with god (January 2021)

Idle Hands (August 2020)

The Almost-Children (May 2019)

Preacher Sam (September 2019)

Bury The Lead (September 2018)

Parable of Pronouns (January 2018)

Praise for *Ghost Girls and Rabbits*

"Brutally silent and unflinchingly loud. With barely a line of dialogue, in *Ghost Girls and Rabbits* the voices of Missing and Murdered Indigenous Women scream to be heard, and Cassondra Windwalker says their names." –**Lindy Ryan**, Bram Stoker Award-nominated author of *Bless Your Heart*

"Cassondra Windwalker's *Ghost Girls and Rabbits* draws you into a mystical tangle of anguish and devotion from the very first page, weaving its way into your heart as you travel alongside the women it portrays, heartbroken yet hopeful, ensnared yet compassionate. This novel shines a light on the epidemic of missing and murdered indigenous women and girls, exploring the desperation of those left behind and their frustration at existing in a world that does not recognize their pain or properly acknowledge the very issue itself. In *Ghost Girls and Rabbits* the reader explores this world through an entrancing lens of lore and the enduring bond forged between two wandering souls." - **Elizabeth Devecchi**, author of *A Whisper in the Dark*

Praise for Other Cassondra Windwalker Titles

"A powerful work of literary, poetical and lyrical fiction, all rolled into one relatively short book, compelling and original, which pushes the buttons for just about every human emotion, then turns each and every scenario on its head and walks away, leaving the reader to dissemble and rearrange their true feelings about the whole spectrum of events and their ensuing tragic consequences." – **Yvonne G**, Goodreads

"Haunting, heartrending and utterly brilliant!" – **Bridget**, Goodreads

"This book is a triumph. Only the best authors give me this feeling, and Cassondra Windwalker is one of them." – **Tiffany Meuret**, author of *A Flood of Posies* and *Little Bird*

"Consistently one of the most compelling writers I know." – **Lisa Alletson**, author of *Good Mother Lizard*

"Cassondra has her hand on the heart of the human condition." – **Lisa De Castro**, author of *Margot*, *The Beauty of Decay*, and *The Girls of Songwood*

"This is such a sweeping but intimate fable, I scarcely feel I've the literary chops to accurately express how beautiful and poignant it was. I've rarely read a modern fantasy with a firmer grasp of a 'language as a living being' ethos, and I don't know if I ever will again." – **L.M. Riviere**, author of *The Innisfail Cycle*

"Her ability to navigate the emotional terrain of betrayal, heartbreak, and tragedy is impressive, but the attention to detail in the narrative structure of the story is nothing short of remarkable." – **Lionel Ray Green**, Horror Tree

"Heartbreaking, harrowing…brilliantly done." – **Isabella**, NetGalley

YEAR ONE
Mary Nelson

The seal pup blinked, mewing piteously against the dim light that must have felt as harsh as the sun. Mary moved quickly. Panic would set in any moment now, and the creature could injure them both in her terror.

The pup resisted Mary's powerful embrace in a spasm of shuddering and struggling that finally subsided into sobbing. Mary stroked the long black hair that she had so recently braided and beaded with elaborate care, lamenting its tangled and sweaty state. She'd known the pup would fight against her confines, but there'd been nowhere to go in the cramped freezer that Mary had buried in a shallow trench outside of Juneau. Still, she'd hoped that some of her training would have stuck with the young one. If she had just remained calm and patient, she would have saved herself much grief. Mary supposed she couldn't blame the pup for fearing the worst when she'd awoken in the dark and the damp.

Gently Mary dislodged the stuffed rabbit toy clenched in the pup's shaking hands. The reluctance with which she surrendered it reassured Mary that the rabbit served its intended purpose. She hadn't wanted to leave the pup all alone in what must have felt like a coffin. The rabbit had been a promise, an unspoken oath that Mary would return, that the dark cold hours would not last forever.

Oddly, though, the seal pup's fear was a comfort to Mary. Perhaps her own beautiful Ryska had awoken in the same darkness and cold and wet that had sealed up this pup. Perhaps Ryska, too, had lain entombed in the earth for long hours of horror and anguish. Had she tried to dig herself free till her fingers bled, like this one? Had she screamed and wept and pled till her throat was raw, like the seal pup?

The questions clawed at Mary, reopening old ruts dug so deep they no longer bled, but today she welcomed the tearing sensation. How many nights had she lain shivering on top of her sheets, refusing the comfort of even a blanket while her daughter might be cold and uncovered out on the muskeg? How many times had she torn at her skin under the searing shower water, as if she could wash herself free of whatever wounds and bruises her daughter endured? How many dawns had she watched with aching eyes, praying that this day's light would finally illuminate Ryska's last steps?

But they'd never found Ryska. Still, not today, not ten years later. Mary never so much as gathered her baby's bones. She hadn't been able to pull her child into her arms and tell her lies about how she was going to be all right now, promise her she would never be hurt again. She hadn't been able to ease that awful mindless fear she now saw gleaming in this seal pup's eyes, hadn't been able to soothe a single ache—hadn't been able to sit by her side till her eyes closed and hold her hand through the long night of terrors.

So, Mary's spirit sighed deeply as those tired old questions dug in their talons. She breathed into the pain, welcomed it. This she could heal. This she could soothe. This she could comfort.

She'd known this stage would take the longest. The seal pup would fight. Mary didn't take it personally. It was simply the creature's nature. Beasts fought. They fought for food, for survival, for power, for dominance. Mary would have to allow the pup to fight until she couldn't fight any more. Then, and only then, could Mary teach the creature that she alone could provide all those desires. Once, in another life, the pup had known that, and her reliance on Mary had been absolute. But this little detour into a buried coffin, awakening completely isolated from the life she'd known before, would startle that understanding out of her. Mary would have to begin again.

That was okay. Mary loved the little seal pup more than she had ever loved anyone but Ryska. However long it took, Mary would remind the pup of who her true protector was. Training was always harder on the trainer than on the trainee. The pup would rebel; she'd beg and plead and argue and cajole, but Mary had to remain firm. She had to do the hard thing, for the good of the pup, for the good of Ryska. For the good of all the missing and murdered little girls out there on the tundra and in the swamp, all the lost ones nobody looked for anymore.

Three days without food had weakened the pup, although of course Mary had ensured that she had plenty of water. If the pup had been thinking, she'd have realized that the hydration pack and oxygen meant that someone was coming back for her. There'd been no need to panic. But Mary supposed some instincts were hardwired. She liked to think that in the same situation, she'd have kept her cool, but maybe that was unfair.

The important thing now was that the pup didn't have energy for much of a fight. Although Mary suspected she'd be able to take her even on a good day. Mary was never inclined to fight the biology of her Russian and Aleut ancestors, preferring to play to her strengths. A home gym helped transform her natural stocky build into powerful muscles. When Ryska disappeared, Mary had kept her Malamute for when she came home, walking it several miles a day. When the poor beast died without ever seeing its mistress again, Mary had maintained her walking schedule. This little seal pup was much more a creature of her time, consumed by appearances and defined entirely by the sleekness of her form. The pup was pretty and easily dressed in costume—Mary knew better than to dignify the pup's performances by calling the calculated frippery regalia—but she was hardly survivor material.

That was why the pup needed Mary. And why, just now, the pup didn't stand a chance.

Mary wasn't worried that the pup would escape. Out here, there was no escape. Only a variety of deaths from which to choose. Mary had been careful to empty the cabin of all but two changes of clothes, and neither of those too warm. The only shoes here were her own, a sturdy pair of waterproof boots by the front door. No coat, no hat, no gloves besides those she'd be taking back out with her when she left. Alaska in November was already bitterly cold.

Likely—although not necessarily—the bears were settling in to hibernation, but the wolves were still about. Even so, the biggest predator here was Alaska itself. In a few weeks, the road Mary had bumped in on would be inaccessible except by snowmobile. Forest and swamp crawled endlessly over the land in every direction. One misstep, one stumble, and the earth itself would swallow you alive. In a few months, Mary knew, the land would spring to life, an incredible effusion of color and power and energy, fed by the endless rot and recycling of the dead.

So, for the pup's own safety, Mary had to restrain her. Otherwise she'd go charging out into that white wilderness against all reason, and Mary would have to go drag her back. She didn't have the time for that, not now, with investigators from every imaginable agency breathing down her neck. Even these few hours away from the city might be tricky to explain if anyone bothered to look too closely.

The pup was filthy, of course. She'd been stewing in her own waste and sweat for three days now. But as much as Mary wanted to clean her up, that would have to wait. However domesticated the pup once was, she'd reverted to feral now. The piteous bleats emitting from the creature's inflamed throat tore at Mary's heart, but she hardened herself. Breaking a wild animal was not a process any thoughtful person would rush. Mary would take the time necessary, regardless of her own personal discomfort. The cabin could be cleaned, the pup could be bathed. But any psychological damage might be permanent. Mary wouldn't risk that.

She debated about the best physical position to leave the pup in. Supine seemed most comfortable, but then, she'd been trapped in something like the fetal position for three days now. It was probably better to have her seated this time. And hopefully Mary'd be back in two days rather than three. She couldn't count on that, though; the investigation might necessitate her staying in town longer than she'd like, so she needed to prepare for any contingency.

She'd gotten the room ready weeks ago. A chair was bolted to the floor in front of the window. Anywhere else, that would have been a risk. Someone might walk by, look in, realize that a woman had been tied to a chair. But not here. And Mary didn't like the idea of the seal pup cooped up with nothing but the walls for company. So, she tied the pup where she could look out the window.

The logistics were complicated, but she'd expected that. She stripped the pup's pants and underwear but pulled on a couple extra pairs of socks. The chair had a hole in the seat with a basin below so that excrement would be a little easier to dispose of. And she could burn these clothes. They were thoroughly soiled anyway. Once she had the pup well-secured, Mary pulled out extra blankets from the closet and tied them around the pup with bungee cords and duct tape. She refilled the water reservoir and hung it on the back of the chair, taping the mouthpiece to the pup's shoulder where she could easily tip her head and take a drink.

There was no need to gag her out here, with no one around to hear her screams for miles. Not to mention that her little throat was so raw, even Mary could hardly hear her protests now. The window the pup faced was the only one in the small cabin unobscured by boards. Keeping the structure as tight as possible would help keep it warm and less likely to attract attention on the outside possibility of anyone wandering by. Mary intended to build up the fire and feed the pup before she left, but after that, the pup would have to rely on ambient heat for survival.

Once she'd been broken, of course, Mary could leave her unrestrained so that she could restoke her own fire and feed herself, but that would take a while. At the beginning, things would be hard. But it would all be worth it in the end.

Carefully, Mary propped up the stuffed rabbit on the windowsill. In a different month, she'd have had to worry about its fur fading in the fierce Arctic sun, but not in November, with its two hours of sunlight and its impossibly long sunrises and sunsets. The seal pup's eyes followed the rabbit, and Mary was pleased that she had some comfort to offer the pitiful creature. The pup's cries quieted.

Mary remembered when she'd gotten Ryska that rabbit as if it were yesterday. Memory was a curse, as far as Mary was concerned, as poisonous and bitter in its wealth as in its paucity. Some days she lost entirely to the rooms of her mind, searching out every corner, capturing every fleck of dust in her hands, panic-stricken in her endeavor to preserve and hold any recollection of Ryska she could find. How as an infant she'd stretched for a full ten minutes before opening her eyes every morning, the intent way she pursed her lips when coloring pages, the resentment in her flashing eyes and drawn brows as her mother told her goodbye before leaving on yet another work trip. The arguments over boys, the unrestrained delight when her mother cooked her favorite fried halibut for dinner, the discordance between the careful paint of a child trying too hard to look like a woman and the reckless ruin of the tracks in her tender young arms. Some days Mary starved for every moment, however ugly and painful it had been, resented every story she'd forgotten.

Other days, Mary wished Ryska would quietly retire into the fog that lingered always on the edges of her mind, wished all that beauty and wonder and hope would follow pain and fear and grief into the great grey place and never return.

But fog and forgetfulness and fear were luxuries Mary didn't have. She wouldn't wish her position on anyone, but here she was. Whether she liked it or not, she was the only chance her daughter had, the only chance this little seal pup had, the only chance so many girls had to be remembered. To be named.

Absently she patted her vest pocket. There, against her heart, lay tucked a handwritten list, names of all the native women missing and murdered in Alaska since Ryska had disappeared. Even that was only a fraction of their numbers, but she could only do what she could do. Every night, Mary whispered their names to the stars. Perhaps when she was dead, then she could forget. For today, she had to remember.

She'd been at the airport, on yet another trip away. Alaska was the size of a small country, much of it inaccessible by any roads. Puddle-jumpers were as casual a conveyance to her as taxis were to New Yorkers. But however everyday the need for travel might be, her daughter never understood when mama left her behind.

Mary'd been on the hunt for a decent cup of coffee—tea would have been better, but she knew better than to drink airport tea. Coffee, at least, they couldn't mess up. She hoped. The fluffy-eared little brown rabbit had caught her eye as she sailed past the touristy gift shop. At ten, Ryska was too old for stuffed animals, but Mary couldn't resist. Something in the bright plastic eyes with their blind hope, the inquisitive tilt of the head, the helplessness of the soft fur, reminded her too immediately of Ryska to be ignored. When she'd made it home and gave Ryska the toy, Ryska had laughed and protested that she wasn't a little girl anymore. But that night, and every night after, Ryska slept with the rabbit tucked up under her chin. Even at eighteen, when she'd stumble home raccoon-eyed and sour-breathed and bitter-tongued, Mary would find her splayed on the sheets, the rabbit clutched against her as if it held the last breaths of the soul Ryska still wanted to save.

On an impulse, Mary turned the rabbit so that it faced out the window, too, instead of looking back at the seal pup tied up and taped up in blankets and cords on the chair. Perhaps the two of them would catch first sight of Ryska's return through the dusty glass.

Food. She needed to feed the pup, and then she needed to leave and get back to her house and the investigation as quickly as she could.

She hadn't been sure what would be best. Between trauma and fear and a three-day empty stomach, she didn't want the pup throwing up what little sustenance she got. So she kept it simple. Warm oatmeal with a bit of milk and butter and cinnamon. Enough to keep the pup functional and comfortable, but not so much to upset her stomach. She'd be plenty hungry again by the time Mary made it back, but that was all to the good. Hunger was a great teacher. Like pain. Like loneliness.

Rebellion stirred in the pup's eyes as Mary carefully spooned the oatmeal into her open mouth, but as expected, appetite outweighed angst. Already the pup was learning. She needed the food more than she needed to make a statement, and so she ate. Mary made a large cup of sweet hot tea, topped with cream. She cooled it carefully, just enough, before offering it to the pup with a straw. She had to pull back several times, coaxing the pup to slow her fierce, thirsty draws for the sugary brew.

As she'd anticipated, the pup called out pitifully as she left, but Mary set her shoulders and turned her back, refusing to allow her steps to slow. Weakness on her part would only do the pup harm in the long run.

Even though their ignorance was crucial to the long-term success of her plan, the ease with which she deflected the investigators' interest discouraged her mightily. She tried, with mixed results, not to be resentful of how much more interest the seal pup's disappearance garnered than Ryska's had. That was the whole point, after all: to use the platform that she had so carefully constructed for her pup to propel the epidemic violence against native women into the public arena. To create a story so big even the most disinterestedly racist media couldn't ignore it, so big even the most ignorant citizens were touched.

She kept vodka on her tongue so Ryska's name wouldn't stick there. She needed to say it, aloud, often, as if it had power and weight of its own, not as if it were ash clinging to the roof of her mouth. And all the lovely newspeople and podcasters with their eyeliner and plastic hair and poreless skin were careful to consult their notes and ask the right questions so that Ryska and the pup were often pictured right alongside each other, their names inextricably linked in the new myth Mary was writing for them.

Mary knew how sympathetic the two girls looked, frozen in beautiful young smiles. She worked hard for that image, insisted on using those two photographs for every media appearance, every social media posting. The seal pup with her deliberate blend of inoffensive Native imagery—delicately beaded braids, unostentatious jewelry, makeup designed to accentuate her cheekbones and her sleek brown skin—and clear political savvy that promised economic return for every lip-service offered. The laughing young Ryska, with windblown hair under a fur hood, round cheeks and narrow eyes and unaffected innocence. Opposite ends of every spectrum but one, and in that one they shared a common fate. Mary wanted people to wonder why. She needed people to ask the question. Why were native women so much more at risk of disappearing and so much less likely to be found?

Mary knew the truth behind those photos. She knew all the seal pup's self-doubts, her hungry ambition, her inane idealism. How her willingness to trade on absolutely anything to get ahead, including her identity, was still somehow an outgrowth of her deep-seated desire to do good. She knew that the Ryska in that photo had been lost long before she disappeared, that one abusive man and too many drugs had stained that innocence more deeply than any mother's hands could launder out.

But media and the people they fed had no taste for truth. They wanted a story like Raven would tell. Raven, whose gift for yarn-spinning was so great that even with a beak still bloodstained from the battlefield, she could craft mythology from misery, glory from spilled guts and greed. And Mary would give it to them.

She didn't care what color Ryska's skin was by the time she made it home. She didn't care how many game trails her daughter had wandered before some hunter snatched her away. She only wanted her home. She wanted to cup her baby's face in her palm. She wanted to brush back the sweaty hair and calm the pounding heart. To hear her daughter's voice, one more time, no matter how hoarse.

If the seal pup had to endure a few dark days to bring Ryska home, so be it. In her heart, Mary knew that the seal pup would understand in the end. How many long nights had she and the pup discussed this very issue, how many meetings had they held with law enforcement agencies and advocacy groups, searching for answers and brainstorming for solutions? The tagline of "missing and murdered indigenous women" had been one of the easiest platforms on which the pup raised her Athabascan flag and drove native voters to the polls. And however adeptly the pup had been willing to use the issue, Mary knew that she was sincere in her desire to make a difference.

Now, thanks to Mary, she could.

Mary had to keep reminding herself of that over the following weeks. She wasn't sure whether she should be dismayed or delighted at how difficult the little pup was to break. The poor creature didn't understand her fight was futile and only hurt herself. Still, Mary couldn't help but admire the fortitude and strength of spirit that kept the pup throwing herself against the wall. In the long run, perhaps that resiliency would allow the pup to thrive in her new identity. Or perhaps it would only shatter her brain. Mary wasn't sure. All she could do was stay the course and hope for the best.

Mary knew her little pup was disconnected from her spirit. Always had been. The pup longed after a deeper existence, but in practice, her greed snatched at the easiest prize first. She knew her history and could recount the simplest stories of her people, the ones white people thought of as metaphorical. She liked to put on leather and fur and contrast her dark skin with that of old white men in the Capitol. But she shied away from slow nights and long silences. Now the pup had nothing else. She would meet her spirit, or she would languish.

Two weeks passed before Mary could even clean the pup. Every time she attempted to untie more than one limb at a time, the pup flew into a rage. Useless, of course, as she only grew weaker and weaker with each successive attempt. The cabin reeked of filth. But Mary was patient.

The pup still tried to communicate, even as Mary laid her out and carefully sponged her bare flesh with warm, soapy, scented water. Mary could see the pup fighting to resist the allure of comfort, the relief of sensation that didn't bring pain. But it was useless. No matter the circumstance, pleasure was still pleasure.

Despite herself, Mary regretted the shame she saw creep into the pup's gaze before she lowered her long-lashed lids. She knew too well the shame of unwelcome pleasure herself. The man who put Ryska in her belly, all those years ago, had been insistent on her pleasure, too. Somehow that had been more awful than the violence, when she'd learned that her own body could betray her even while her mind fought. It had been no hardship to resist pleasure after that.

She hadn't intended to force that humiliation on the pup, but she realized now it was inevitable. The creature simply fought too hard. If this was it took to break her, to still her fight, to soothe her spirit, so be it.

So Mary cleaned the skin, washed the hair and dried it with a soft towel. She even brushed the pup's teeth, rinsed out her mouth. Took her out to the outhouse and allowed her to relieve herself like a person would. When she brought the pup back into the warm firelit cabin and tied her back to the chair, rewrapped her in the blankets and cords and tape, the pup hung her head and sobbed as she had not done since Mary dug her out of the ground.

Almost, then. They were getting closer to success.

The whole process, from burial to resurrection to rebirth, took three months, much longer than Mary had hoped. Once complete, though, the transformation was beautiful to behold.

Mary untied the pup, one limb at a time, carefully massaging and exercising each one before moving on to the next. The pup was silent, her eyes fixed on Mary's face. Once free, she waited for Mary's nod before sliding to the floor. She crawled across the cabin, slowly retrieved the rabbit from its sentinel position in the window, and then scuttled to the cheerfully crackling fire. Mary took her time even now, aware of how dangerous too much freedom could be, if given too soon.

She would leave the pup for a day or two at a time, unrestrained. Firewood was stacked in a shelter outside. Mary took the socks away at first, so the pup had to trudge out barefoot in the snow to retrieve more fuel. For this stage, Mary emptied the cabin of its blankets. The pup had a mattress, a pillow, and a pair of panties. If she wanted to stay warm, she had to keep the fire stoked and stay close.

Once she proved herself trustworthy, the pup earned back a pair of socks. It didn't take as long as Mary feared. Cold was a brutal keeper. Tears started to Mary's eyes at the helpless joy in the seal pup's face as she pulled the socks over her aching feet, but Mary ruthlessly blinked them away. Soon enough the pup would have all she needed. What she needed now was for Mary to stay strong and take good care of her.

The next week she brought the pup a long-sleeved t-shirt. Last of all a pair of grey sweatpants, thick and soft. The pup gripped her hand and pressed desperate kisses to Mary's palm before tucking herself up into a fetal position in front of the fire, her hands rubbing her cotton-enclosed calves as if she'd never been so happy in her life.

Vigilance was key. Even now, Mary only left enough food and fuel for half of the time she would be gone. She took the axe with her so that the pup couldn't do more for herself than gather twigs, most of which were too damp to burn. The pup might be weak, but she was still canny and clever. Mary wouldn't underestimate her, broken or not. The pup's complete dependence was key.

The return of the sun and the long hot days of summer proved too much of a stimulant for the pup's facile mind. One day in August, prompted by some mysterious maternal stirring, Mary returned to the cabin a day early.

The pup was gone.

She wasn't difficult to track, but the danger was too dire for Mary to ignore. She stripped the pup of all her hard-worn clothes and broke both her legs.

Absolutely gutted, Mary set about the process of taming the pup all over. She didn't suppose children ever understood how their parents suffered on their behalf until they had children of their own. The year that followed was a long, wretched, torturous affair that reminded Mary of Ryska's sixteenth year.

But Mary didn't regret a moment. For Ryska, for the seal pup, she would do whatever it took.

YEAR ONE
Noni Begay

Lord, her head hurt. Noni shifted awkwardly, her stomach lurching as terror surged over her aching limbs. Something was terribly wrong.

She strained her eyes, even stretching her lids with her fingers to ensure they were really open, but the darkness around her was a physical thing, a huge black beast wrapping its limbs around her and swallowing her head whole in its steamy maw. Frantically she tried to propel herself up, out of whatever horror she'd fallen into, but her cramped arms and legs beat uselessly against walls around her, above her, below her.

She was in a box.

She sucked in a breath, choking on a scream she fiercely battened down. It was a dream. It had to be a dream. Only a dream.

How many times had she woken in a sweat, running through a darkness that never lifted, reaching for a door that never met her fingers? A lightless, airless hallway that became eternal limbo. This was just another nightmare.

Except here, her fingers met nothing but doors, doors that refused to give way. Her knees were folded nearly to her chin; she could only stretch a few inches more. If she slid down, she could raise her head. Wrestling against panic, she scrambled and fought to tangle and untangle her limbs, managing at last to get her legs underneath her and using her bent shoulders to press against the roof of her prison with all her strength, but it didn't give.

How did she even know that was up? What if she were buried upside down, deep in the belly of the earth? Her breath sawed in and out of her chest till she thought her breastbone would wrench apart.

No. No, that was nonsense. Gravity still applied, no matter where she was. She knew up from down.

She pushed again and again and again, grunting and struggling to gain some leverage from her knees, but nothing moved. Finally she began the laborious process of shifting her limbs back to their former position. As she settled, panting, into her narrow corner, she became aware of air blowing across her face, of the soft hum of a motor. Groping across the small space, her fingers encountered a small fan bolted to the top of her box.

Eventually it would occur to her that someone wanted her to survive, at least for a while, but in the moment, it was only a way out, a corridor to open air and room to stretch. She clawed and tugged at it, screaming into its caged blades for help, for someone, for anyone. Her fury subsided in an instant when she realized she might just break it, might destroy her only source of air. Fear returned, all-consuming and intense, and she shrank back, howling herself raw till mad panic subsided into exhaustion.

What was happening? Somehow she had been sucked into a nightmare. She'd misstepped, taken one step too many into the quicksand, one step too near the edge of some invisible cliff, and now she'd fallen past the point of return. Who could have done this?

She counted seconds as she breathed in and out, deciding with cold clarity that she would rather die calm than in a panic. The last thing she remembered was driving down the dirt roads that snaked from ocean to forest to ocean again with Mary at the wheel.

Three nights after their great triumph. Together they'd accomplished the impossible, fending off the patriarchal bigots and misogynists of Alaskan politics and seducing them by turns, convincing both big oil and big fish that a Native Alaskan senator would prove both poster-girl for conservationists and puppet for deep-pocketed interest groups. It had hardly been a landslide, but it had been a win, and now Alaska's first Native senator would be on her way to Washington.

Would have been.

Noni clutched her skull, trying to make sense of her scattered memories amid the throbbing pain in her temples. Mary had been her staunchest, fiercest advocate. Almost from the first moment she met the stocky, stoic-faced campaign manager, Noni trusted her not just with her career but with her heart. Trust was an illusion, even in the small arena of state politics, but Mary was different. They'd been connected. Both Native, though Noni hailed from the interior Athabascans and Mary was a coastal Aleut. Both women in a world where female statesmen were defined by their ability to balance work with children and judged by their pantsuits and headbands. More than mere alliance had bound them, though. Somehow Mary Nelson had become a mother to Noni, a best friend, a defender.

And Mary Nelson was no softie. She had a hard-won reputation for navigating the churning rivers of corruption and clapbacks with a determined oar. Allies lauded her and enemies sought her. She'd become a fixture in state politics, a reliable crafter of deals who actually got things done while public faces insisted on principle and raked in votes. She'd seen many fresh-faced young idealists come and go, but she recognized something stronger and fiercer in Noni Begay.

Noni possessed that rare combination of passionate conviction and cold-eyed pragmatism that had typified the young Mary, too. But where Mary had been discounted, Noni was camera-ready and more than willing to exploit it. With Mary's help, she mastered the demographics: stark, sleek business suits to appease the women, with just enough collarbone and knee to draw in the men. She shook hands like a business mogul but wore braids like a protester. She played to every stereotype she could find without an ounce of remorse. The world wanted to put her in a box? Fine. She'd own the box and turn it into a podium.

But now she might die in a box, and there was only one person who could have put her there.

Mary Nelson.

Even as her mind rebelled, she knew there was no other possibility. The night was muddy in her mind, and she realized there must have been something in the bottled iced tea Mary offered her when she'd climbed in the vehicle. Mary had been distraught—or so Noni thought. The older woman had been tearful, angry, and hopeful by turns, talking about her missing daughter Ryska. Her certainty that Noni's win two days before would be the final catalyst to finding her.

Noni had never met Ryska. Mary's daughter had been missing for ten years, long before Noni had crossed paths with her mother. But her absence was an unspoken and constant truth between them. The issue of missing and murdered indigenous women on the North American continent had been the signal platform of Noni's campaign. It was hard for anyone to be unmoved by the plight of the families left behind or the faces of the lost.

On the surface, the issue was innocuous enough to be unassailable. No one could argue with the numbers. And the old white man on the other side of the aisle could hardly advocate as sympathetically as a beautiful young woman with dark skin and long black hair. The irony, of course, was that the same systemic bigotry and misogyny that oiled American politics had created the crisis. To attack one necessarily meant to attack the other. But for now, Noni was content to hold up photos of the missing and sit with the bereaved. Once she got to Washington, real change could begin.

That's what Mary had been counting on. Or so Noni had thought. They'd been united in their vision, willing to play whatever parts were required to win a position of enough power to affect a difference. Noni couldn't imagine when things had changed, what Mary's motivation could be. Why the woman she trusted most in the world, besides her own mother, would nail her up in a box of nightmarish anguish and leave her there.

But the last thing she remembered was Mary's slurred voice, saying Ryska's name.

Could they both have been attacked, and she didn't remember it? Could Mary be locked up in a box of her own? She seized on the idea, desperate for hope. Maybe she wasn't alone. Maybe Mary could hear her. Maybe Mary had been unconscious when Noni screamed before.

She felt it unwinding from her throat again, a howling keen that sometimes took the form of a name or a word and sometimes only unwound and unwound endlessly into the darkness. She lost track of the shapes of the sound and the ragged breaths feeding them, lost track of sense and reason, lost track of when she screamed and when she slept. Every joint, every inch of skin burned with pain, her nails bled, her hair clumped in her hands. Time passed and time went nowhere at all.

By the time her tiny universe moved around her, bumping and rattling her bruised body in its invisible confines, she had no voice left at all. Terror, that she'd thought impossible to revive from its rancid sludge, stirred and subsided and stirred again as this rocking motion became her new eternity. Something out there, if there still was an out there, was changing, but here in the darkness, all was the same.

She'd tried telling herself stories for a while. At first, they were only fairy-tales: *they're looking for you, they'll find you, they'll save you.* Soon she graduated to truer tales. The week before the election, news crews had videotaped her reading Alaska Native folktales to elementary school students: perfectly acceptable, non-threatening theatre for a female candidate. She supposed she'd learned the same stories when she was their age, but they'd long since been banished in place of the history and science and law she'd studied at university.

Now, though, they offered comfort for a while. She imagined Raven discovering her plight, outwitting her captor, freeing her from this blighted darkness that would not lift. She told herself she was *K'i-talqani*, transformer and defeater. Instead of metamorphosizing her enemy into a shape she could defeat, she would metamorphosize herself. She pictured herself shrinking, folding in on herself in thousands of iterations till she emerged tiny and fierce, hard-shelled and many-legged, to scurry along these walls and out through the cruel freedom of the fan's corridor to open air.

She felt warm sunshine blazing along her black shell, felt herself unfolding again into woman, into spirit, into light, then back into beaver, like *K'i-talqani* himself. She would be Beaver Woman, never again bounded by land or water or men. She would leave words and reason behind. She would swim in the water, build with wood, feel fish-flesh burst between her teeth. She would rise beneath the sweet and sharp caresses of the free wind, not this continual rasp of blown air that left her raw and gasping. She would walk the swampy woods where lay hidden and discarded the bodies of her former sisters. She would carry their names in her fur.

But by the time her world went still again, she'd lost track of stories, too. When light blazed across her too-human body, she only recounted lists in her head: noble gases, States of the Union, tribes of the Pacific Northwest, the wives of Henry VIII, square roots. Anything to keep her limbs from spasming into their habitual panic.

She tried to scream despite herself when the light scraped relentlessly across her wounded eyes and skin, though her throat only contracted raw against itself. As strong arms lifted her out, agony scratched and clawed its way along her bones, burst through her locked muscles, and tears streamed unfelt down her cheeks. Even so, she couldn't restrain herself from the instinctive fight, flapping uselessly at the figure who handled her with such efficient dispatch and disdain.

When her eyes finally adjusted to the light, her gaze seized on the face near hers: Mary Nelson. Mary, Mary, her mother of spirit, her friend, her savior.

All the numbers and names that had held her mind stitched together vanished, and she reached for Mary in pathetic gratitude. Too swiftly, horror descended in its place as Mary gazed back at her with empty eyes and blank face. However Noni tried, she couldn't persuade Mary to speak, to answer her questions, to say her name. Hard hands stretched her legs out straight as they screamed in protest, then as remorselessly tied them to the legs of a wooden chair. Blood burned like fire through her body before pooling into a new anguish as she was bound upright in front of a curtainless window.

She could hardly blink. Starved for images, for light, her hungry retinas strained against the air, her lids raised in perpetual surprise as she gazed and gazed and gazed. Her brain had forgotten how to process the information, and shapes and lines and colors fell in a scrambled kaleidoscope through her consciousness as she struggled to interpret them. Her nerves spasmed and shuddered as they simultaneously fought to absorb and limit sensation.

Wood. Cold. Smoke. Red. Soft. Hard. Warm sticky sugar on her tongue. Pain.

Pain. Pain. Pain.

Suddenly Noni became aware of a withdrawal in the air around her, some premonition of absence. She craned her aching neck, but she could no longer find Mary's vacant gaze. The last sound she heard was a door scraping shut, some sort of hollow wooden sound falling in a thud.

Nonononononono….

Stillness descended over her again, a different stillness than she'd suffered in her box, but a stillness all the same. How could Mary leave her? Uselessly, weakly, she strained against her bonds, but to no purpose. She'd been taped into a different shape than the one she'd been forced to hold for—how long? Days? Weeks? Years?—but the new shape was no more forgiving than the old one. Her stomach cramped without warning, immediately expelling its meager contents into the basin under her chair.

No pants. Socks. Some sort of warm, soft fabric wrapped around her torso. Ill-fitting mittens pulled over her stiff fingers. A knit hat tugged over her ears. She catalogued her new wardrobe as if it were a periodic table, pulling herself out of the burgeoning panic by recounting what was real. At least, she thought it was real. She hoped it was real.

Maybe she was still curled up in that box of darkness like a vine in its unbroken seed. Maybe all of this was only as real as the river where Beaver Woman fished and built her home.

No. Not even her tortured mind would conjure a reality in which her friend became her tormenter. Somehow, this had to be real.

That was too awful to contemplate. Helplessly she returned to her archival. She turned her head as far as she could to the left and began ordering every object in her mind: the rough-cut shelves, the tin teapot, the wood stove, the fireplace, the slightly-less-than-square window, the stand of trees across the muskeg, more shelves, coat hooks without coats, a narrow bed that taunted her with its promise of decadence, the impossible luxury of stretching her limbs full length.

The fire burned out so quickly, too quickly. Cold crept in through the corners and cornices. Shivers set in, and soon her muscles ached with the effort. Her bare thighs turned bright red in the icy room, and she tried to focus on her toes inside the wool socks, wiggling them against the fabric and imagining their meager heat could spread. One of her mittens fell off, and she opened and closed her hand spasmodically, trying desperately to keep circulation active. She turned her head left to right in slow, incessant tabulation of her paltry existence. Now she didn't tally anything so large and clumsy as a shelf or a pan. She followed the topography of wood grain in every uneven log, examined the crevasses and couloirs of the grimy chinking, made friends of the lint adrift in the musty air and became teller of their adventures as they journeyed. She named her new agonies, made strangers of her own flesh and bones till she could rejoin them without torment.

November days in Alaska were only noncommittal nights. Bleary grey sunlight peered in the window occasionally, but darkness was the more faithful friend. Icy rains surged and receded against the ragged cabin walls. Noni supposed she should be grateful it wasn't more snow and ice—if the temperatures sank lower, she might suffer actual frostbite. But gratitude was as distant as resignation. Mary showed up periodically, or at least this weird inhuman husk that wore Mary's face as casually as a coat.

The Mary-monster never spoke a word. Never indicated by so much as a flicker of her gaze that she understood anything Noni said. She'd give Noni a chance, untie her bonds, stretch out her arms, rub her skin, but at the first sign of resistance, she simply retied the knots. Between the long, forced immobility, cold, hunger, and exhaustion, Noni was no match for the much stronger woman.

Black to grey to black again, rainfall and silence and rainfall, and at last Noni forced her inner fight into submission. She couldn't win by brute force; she couldn't persuade this woman with no ears. Submission was the only rebellion she had left.

She readied herself for the violation in her days of reprieve—or days of suffocating isolation; she no longer knew which was which. She sang long songs to her muscles, urging them to be still and grow strong. She told stories to her bones, stories of long winters and stunning, powerful springs. She was ready, she thought; she could yield now to rise later.

But the cost. Oh, the cost was so much higher than she had figured.

The Mary-monster nodded approvingly at her flaccid limbs and downcast eyes when she untied her this time. She set her square shoulder under Noni's weak arm and half-carried her to the bed whose promised comfort had tormented Noni for what now felt like years. Formless moans escaped her lips unbidden as she sank into the deliciously soft warmth of the fire-heated blankets. Mary warmed a pot of water on the woodstove and gently washed Noni's body free of the filth and grime and sweat that coated her skin and hair. Despite herself, Noni wept with gratitude as the warmth sank into her bones and pleasure beyond anything she could have imagined flooded her starved senses.

Unexpectedly, shame suffused her. She despised herself as a pathetic sniveling beast desperate for any kind touch, any meager delight. But no amount of humiliation, no choking embarrassment was powerful enough to prompt her to rebellion now. She wanted to tell herself this submission was only a pretense, a farce she had to uphold until she regained strength enough to fight, but she knew better. In this moment, for this brief respite from agony, she would do anything to stay in the blankets, to luxuriate in the decadence of fully extended limbs, to not feel the wooden frame of the chair cutting into her hipbones.

Alone in the cabin, she could remind herself of who she was, but when Mary was there, with her food and warmth and solace, Noni all but forgot her own name. Mary still didn't speak to her, no matter how Noni pleaded, so eventually Noni stopped trying. Now, with warm soapy water bathing her skin and the soft spines of the hairbrush massaging her scalp, she could only stare into Mary's vacant eyes, clinging to the reflection of herself she saw there.

The next few weeks were a new and terrible exercise in deprivation. Noni was no longer left tied to the chair that had taken on the aspect of some ghastly instrument of torture, but Mary took with her all those lovely blankets and all Noni's clothes but her panties. Noni had to scramble bare footed in the cold to retrieve wood for the fire and stay huddled on its hearth. She would let it burn down as far as she dared and then dart outside to carry as much wood as she could at a time. She never knew exactly when Mary would return, so she rationed out her meager food as best she could. Cold and hunger became the definition of her existence, the rough edges of the map of her mind that seemed forever to be shrinking.

Piece by piece, Mary restored her clothing to her, and Noni hated herself more each time for the desperate thankfulness with which she received every scrap of cloth. Sometimes she couldn't remember if she played docile because she wanted her freedom or if she only wanted more food, more clothes, another blanket. Maybe she wasn't playing anymore. Maybe docility was all that remained.

During Mary's absences, Noni filled her small wooden world with language. She told stories to the ragged stuffed rabbit as it sat in the window or at night when they huddled together on the narrow bed. She began venturing outside, taking words with her like a leash that ensured she could safely return to the cabin cage that had become her only refuge. She reminded herself aloud of the names of every blooming flower, every weird and colorful mushroom, every stalwart tree forming a rough ring around her small clearing. She spoke to the mud and asked questions of the birds and butterflies and mosquitoes. When she tired, she followed the trail of dropped syllables back to the cabin and promised herself the corners there collected her stories along the shimmering strands of light pretending to be cobwebs.

But when Mary returned, language drained from the air like stardust into a black hole. Silence pushed between the chinked logs and lay piled like corpses on the floor. Noni's feet felt heavy, her tongue swollen, even as she chewed and swallowed the meals Mary cooked for her. She still tried, sometimes, to force out sounds that reminded her of words Mary would know, but the still stagnancy in Mary's answering gaze convinced her she'd lost the shape of words.

On a warm morning when the soft breezes whispered insistently against the wooden walls of the cabin, Noni left the little rabbit behind. She propped it up in the window where it could watch her go. It was time, she decided. All the words that had been choked out coalesced into a single message echoing through her mind, drowning out every other thought: *run, run, run, runrunrun.*

She didn't know where she was, didn't know what direction might lie help or hope. Growing up in Alaska, she was well aware of the wilderness galloping away in every direction from any tiny outpost of civilization. It would be the easiest thing in the world to get lost mere yards from safety and never approach so much as a game trail before Alaska ate you up. But what was the point of gaining Mary's trust, winning new clothes and new privileges, if she wasn't going to try and escape? If she consented to her own imprisonment, if she gave up, what would be left of her?

She had to go.

She hadn't made it very far into the trees when she heard the rumbling engine that signaled Mary's return on the ATV. What were the chances that her former mentor would return in the very moments of her escape? Surely some wicked spirit had whispered Noni's name into Mary's ear. Fear swelled in her throat, her heart thundering along her veins till she could hardly think, and her spent limbs shook so hard they barely supported her weight.

Panic overtook her, robbing her of any ability to creep and sneak unseen, unheard, through the thick underbrush of the Alaskan rainforest. She charged blindly ahead, smashing through moss-draped tree limbs and stumbling, falling, stumbling again over the tree stumps, rocks, and sinkholes camouflaged in the lush overgrowth. She ended up huddled behind a broad tree trunk, fighting for air, arms wrapped around her knees as if her long black hair could curtain her from Mary's eyes.

When she heard the approaching steps, a weak burst of adrenaline set her back on her feet. Somehow the silence of Mary's approach, her refusal even now to call Noni's name, increased the awful horror of the hunt. But her brief burst of speed couldn't last, and Mary had always been devoted to her personal endurance and strength training. It took mere seconds for Mary to overtake Noni and throw her to the ground.

All her will and dignity stolen by terror, Noni sobbed and pleaded as the stone-faced Mary half-hauled, half-dragged her back to the cabin. She begged forgiveness, begged Mary not to leave her tied up again as the other woman remorselessly bound her back to the dreaded chair. In the window, the little stuffed rabbit kept its back resolutely turned, as if it feared to look upon what came next.

Still, she didn't comprehend what was happening when Mary left her field of vision and returned with a sledgehammer. It wasn't until the back side of the anvil sliced through the air toward her left leg that she began fighting against the ropes in earnest. Pain burst behind her eyes like blood and filled the room with crimson blackness as agony spiraled and swelled through her. She could hear screams rising and falling, felt the wrench in her chest when the successive blows on her right leg forced out the contents of her stomach. The world dipped and spun, blinding her with a meaningless kaleidoscope of colors and shapes till she slowly became aware she'd been dragged back onto the bed. Mary moved around the small cabin kitchen, puttering from task to task as if nothing had happened.

Noni turned her head to the wall as tears streamed unchecked down her face. Her bleary eyes made out the face of the Beaver Woman she'd found in the wood grain months ago. She moved her mouth, tried to form the word, but no sound came. Silence overtook her while pain screamed on and on.

YEAR TWO
Mary Nelson

Rising and falling in a continual cascade of black wings and guttural calls, the cormorants harassed Mary day and night. Black suits and black ink scrawling down the same answers to the same questions again and again. She understood they merely acted according to their nature, but couldn't help resenting how much more they persisted than when Ryska disappeared. That had been the whole point, of course, to force them to do for the seal pup what they hadn't done for her daughter. Even so, she was disappointed by her own success.

She said Ryska's name aloud now as often as she could. With the cormorants had come the coyotes, who had disdained her daughter entirely ten years ago, dismissing her story as the tired old cliché of a red-skinned addict with a white-skinned beater who had gone the way of all such girls. Mary had fought for the one paragraph her daughter merited in the Juneau newspaper, and she'd only gotten that because she fed the coyotes scraps for so long they felt obligated to offer her something.

Absence isn't substance.

Mary remembered the sharp-snouted, black-eyed coyote with the red mouth who'd exasperatedly insisted that there was no story in a Native girl who was simply still gone. As if coyotes cared how much meat was on the bones they scattered on screen for distracted viewers. As if they didn't love to taunt the hungry with promises of sustenance they would never fulfill. Scavengers, all of them, with snarls where smiles should be. She hated them.

She hated the coyotes for counting her daughter as trash, not even worth a few seconds' sniffing. If they'd shown her photo, if they'd told her story, if they'd said her name, surely someone would have come forward with something—anything—that could have helped them find her. Ryska hadn't vanished; she'd been taken, taken by someone who'd hurt her. Maybe—Mary refused to shy away from the thought, ten years after the fact—maybe killed her. Someone knew something. Someone struggled under the weight of guilt, the shackles of lies that wound every year higher up their body.

But that someone never had to face what they'd done. Their family and friends weren't calling Ryska's name, holding up her photograph, searching the swamps and the tundra for her. That someone didn't feel the constant pressure and fear of the hunted beast, chased down by cormorants and coyotes and flushed from every hiding spot. That someone had been able to keep their ordinary life, unhunted and fearless, one among hundreds of rabbit-eaters whose appetites were never sated, whose fires were never quenched, whose bellies were never empty.

Mary hated the cormorants as much as she hated the coyotes. When Ryska was taken, two or three skated in on the wind, took down all her information, and skated as swiftly out, without making so much as a single dive beneath the dark waters. And dark and cold and murky the waters were, Mary knew. She'd been losing pieces of Ryska long before she'd disappeared, to drugs and despair and self-loathing that Mary didn't understand and couldn't heal. She'd been all kinds of broken, her little one, but she'd also been beautiful and vibrant and alive. She'd been worth the space she held on this earth. But the cormorants hadn't thought so. They hadn't wanted to sully their glossy wings in those oily waters where truth lurked. They'd taken to the air and left her daughter gasping her last breath out in the deep.

Mary shook her head, scattering the grief from its heap so the weight was easier to bear. Maybe not. Maybe Ryska had been traded out, traded off, funneled into the sex trade where she still waited and hoped for her mother to come find her. Mary didn't know if that would be better or worse. What was a mother to choose, between wishing her daughter were dead and wishing her daughter were a slave to monsters?

Whichever was true, Mary would bring her daughter home. Ryska would not be lost forever. Her baby had a home, a mother's arm, a name that waited for her still.

Even now, as the anniversary of last year's election and the seal pup's grand exit approached, the cormorants could hardly hide their eagerness to leave this place behind. They'd soared back in, of course, darkening the sky and filling the air with their noise, in time to meet the coyotes and put on a display of urgency and effort. Perhaps they even believed that they'd scare up something new, that some fresh clue would come to light. But Mary saw them when they thought no one was looking, sullen and still in the sun, wings outspread, lids drooping, waiting to shed the weight of water from their feathers. It was no great trick to fool them.

All she had to do was persist. Persist just one moment longer than the cormorants did. Soon they would be back in the air, and she would be back with her seal pup.

She'd had such hopes at first. Irrational, she knew that now. Somehow she'd had the mad idea that in looking for the pup, they'd find her Ryska. They hadn't. The fools hadn't even considered that the two disappearances, ten years apart, might be connected. They'd brushed aside her story and instead focused on political extremists or the seal pup's silly boyfriend. Once again Ryska had been counted as debris.

But the coyotes had a taste for the story at last. The seal pup was so pretty, with her sleek fur and huge dark eyes, her graceful form, and they loved the irony that the Senator who'd been elected while calling on the nation to address the issue of missing and murdered indigenous women had herself fallen into their number. Mary had not only been the seal pup's campaign manager, she'd been her closest friend, and the coyotes delightedly zoomed in on the stoic-faced Aleut with the single tear on her ruddy cheeks. Mary never turned down an interview, and she always took the same two photos—one of Ryska and one of the pup.

She'd lost two daughters, she would tell the coyotes, who would force their painted maws into grotesque imitations of sympathy and gesture to their cameraman to get in closer, closer.

But how many other daughters lay lost along the highways, she would mournfully demand. How many other mothers lay hollow-bellied in their beds every night?

Mary ate at every table the coyotes set: television, YouTube, podcasts, blogs, magazine articles, radio interviews. But their food was sand on her tongue.

The timing was terrible, naturally. The seal pup had staged her little rebellion just two months before the anniversary of her disappearance, and her subsequent care required Mary to travel back and forth far more frequently than she wanted the cormorants to observe. She'd gotten through the first few horrible weeks with no difficulty, before either the cormorants or the coyotes checked their calendars and came circling the carcasses for a quick bite. But once they showed up, she had to curtail her movements, which meant the pup suffered in her absence.

She tried to remind herself that the pup brought this pain on herself, but she could hardly bear it all the same. The hideous bleating sounds the creature made tore at her heart. Consistency, she knew, was key. However much she longed to comfort the poor beast, to ease her pain for this moment, she had to think about what was best for the pup in the long term. A little agony now, and later, when the seal pup was fully broken, they could return to their old companionship, with its sympathy and consolations. To be lenient now would only prolong the pup's suffering, and that she would not do.

Privately, she fretted that her discipline had been too harsh. In the moment, she'd been overcome with terror, all the possible scenarios that could have unraveled. The pup could have been devoured by the bears, brown or black, who roamed unchecked this time of year. She could have gotten lost and wandered until she starved to death or injured herself. She could have plunged down a sinkhole or been consumed by a swamp.

She could have been found, and all Mary's plotting, all her hopes for Ryska, would have been destroyed.

In that moment of panic, no response seemed too severe. She needed to be certain that the pup would be contained. Breaking both her legs had been a gut reaction, like that of a mother knocking her child back from the hot stove.

In retrospect, though, the cost had been higher than she'd anticipated.

The recovery period for two broken legs, even though she'd taken care to break them cleanly and not cause any splintering or spiraling, was months at least. The whole point had been incapacitation, and she'd definitely achieved that. Suddenly, though, her fosterling was much more labor-intensive a project. Luckily for the pup, the worst of her recovery had been in the warmer months, though warm was a relative term. Now that November was upon them, sleeting rain blew against the cabin day and night, and ice clung to the eaves. Mary had taken to piling wood near the front door. The pup still had to drag herself to the door, grab one or two pieces, and drag herself back to the fire, but the exercise was good for her.

Mary decided to wait until Christmas to give her back her clothes. November 28th would be the beginning of Advent, and a perfect occasion to gift the pup with some warm and soft flannels to help keep her comfortable through the long dark months. By then, Mary was confident that the pup would not only have learned the error of her ways but would have come to rely entirely on Mary for all she needed. In the meantime, she had to make do with the blankets Mary had given her and however much of a fire she could manage to keep burning between Mary's visits.

Mary had been mistaken in thinking the pup tame before, and she wasn't going to risk another shortcut. More work for her, but completely worth it in the end. She fed the seal by hand, always bringing the most tasty, delectable treats she could, all the favorite dishes she knew the pup loved. While she was in the cabin, she made sure the fire was well-stoked, roaring high and cheerful. She even brought cinnamon and teakwood scented candles to burn as she stroked the pup's hair after supper until those dark, haunted eyes slid closed at last. She used every sensory pathway she could to lead the pup to safety and comfort in her presence, and in her presence only.

When she left, she took everything with her. Well, almost everything. She left a stash of broth and bread in case she wasn't able to get back when she planned. Two blankets and a pillow. But everything else—extra blankets and pillows, food and candy and candles—she took back with her. The pup had to learn. And only a scant supply of wood, so the pup had to ration her warmth as she had to ration everything else without Mary. Although keeping the fire burning was enough of a chore that limiting the fuel was likely not necessary. Mary hated to think how the pup agonized to keep the fire fed, her damaged legs bumping over the cold wooden floor as she dragged herself along.

As it turned out, the cormorants were disappointingly disinterested in her frequent absences. They made it clear they saw her as little more than another talking head, another would-be politician profiting from someone else's loss. On one hand, Mary could hardly blame them. It was true enough that the seal pup's sudden disappearance had propelled her from the backstage into the house lights. Some Anchorage folks were even making noise about Mary herself running for office. Most notably, the pup's own parents and that long-haired boyfriend of hers.

She supposed she couldn't fault them. From their point of view, she was the person most likely to carry out the pup's own legacy. Most devoted to her causes.

They wouldn't know how she'd despised all the pandering, the posturing the pup had been forced to perform to hold the place she'd earned. The only way a Native woman had managed to win the election was by assuring the good ol' boys who ran the oil and fish businesses that she posed no threat to their economic positions. And no one made a better poster-girl for developers than the much sought-after "person of color." Even the attention that the pup had brought to the issue of missing and murdered indigenous women on the North American continent as a whole, and Alaska in particular, had been totally acceptable as a "women's issue" cloaked in pink underwear and Instagram selfies and caramel-iced lattes.

Like so many lost souls before her, the pup had the best of intentions, and Mary knew she truly believed she could make a difference "once I have the power." As if Washington were somehow lacking in the self-interest and corruption that permeated policies here in the Frozen North. Mary had known all along what the pup hadn't—that she'd have to keep making the same compromises, wearing the same shame, braiding the same beads in Washington as she'd done here, and to little more forward momentum. Mary wouldn't be roped into that rodeo. She knew she was, and who she wouldn't be.

In spite of that, she sometimes dreamed of the pup's triumphant return. How the people would love her. How the coyotes would fall slathering at her feet. How she could surely do anything, accomplish anything, convince anyone, then.

Maybe. But until then, training was paramount.

She tried not to notice the first time the pup called her mama instead of Mary. The pup's voice had long been birdsong in a storm, trembling notes that sometimes caught the ear but more often were torn away in the gusts. That sound, though—that sound caught, and held, and shattered again and again against her heart. For a moment, she could almost imagine the seal pup spoke with a human tongue.

Christ is born, Mama.

How she missed Ryska at Christmastime. Although unorthodox in many ways, Mary and her daughter had clung to the old Russian traditions where they could. They'd delighted in their contempt for the Protestants and the early Christmas and all the commercialism that infected the holiday's customs. Likely some children would have regretted that their friends got to celebrate the holiday two weeks earlier, but not Ryska. Admittedly, she hadn't been as fond of—or as devoted to—the fasting, but she'd gloried in the day itself. She had nothing but pity for her heathen friends with their fat red Santa.

Mary told herself that she was hearing things. Little seals didn't speak in human tongues. But for a moment, as she clasped the pup close in her soft down blanket, she imagined that she did.

Cut my hair, Mama.

Nearly five months had passed since the pup's last rebellion, five long months of pain and rehabilitation and recovery. Many weeks remained until the pup could get her legs back under her without fear of falling. In this time, though, Mary and the pup had grown inexpressibly close. The pup nuzzled her tenderly, her length stretched out trustingly along Mary's own, the warm weight a benediction. Mary ran her fingers through the pup's long locks, now hanging past her waist. Although she'd tried to care for the pup as well as she could under the circumstances, the long months of deprivation and pain had taken their toll. The ends were split, the hair thinning even as it lengthened. Mary could trace a silver hair or two from the pup's scalp.

Perhaps she should cut the pup's hair. Just trim a few inches. She could braid it and bead it and dress it for their Christmas supper, already cooking away on the stove.

January already. Mary could hardly believe this was already their second Christmas night together, and still no sign of Ryska anywhere. Mary pushed down her grief. No need to burden the pup with her sorrow. Let her find joy where she might. Somewhere, somehow, Mary wished desperately that Ryska had some small joys reserved to her, too. That someone was kind to her, if only for a moment.

Christ is born, my darling, my little rabbit, she thought with all the strength in her heart. *Be at peace. I am coming for you. I will find you. Don't give up.*

She stroked the long black hair, rifled the shaggy hands between her fingers.

A haircut would be good.

She gave the pup all the ceremony she would have given Ryska, if those damn cormorants had ever brought her broken little body back. She built up the fire so that the cramped cabin glowed with light and warmth. She stripped away the sweaty flannels and sponged the seal pup's flaccid skin, taking extra care on the sunken legs that had yet to regain their lost muscle. With tender hands, she massaged in the apple butter lotion she'd brought as a gift. She washed the pup's little face with a soft cloth, careful not to get soap in the dark eyes that watched her with such grace in their liquid depths. Finally, she laid the pup back against the basin where she could shampoo and condition the long, greasy hanks that had been neglected for so long.

A wide-toothed comb parted the silky locks, gently found a path through the tangles. She concentrated on the strands sifted between her own strong, rough-skinned fingers, gauging the length. She drew the scissors from her pocket.

The seal became a snake.

The slender, supple body contracted in a smooth blur of motion that staggered Mary, left her reeling, broken loose from her reverie and the vision of Ryska's cold, pale body laid out for washing. Before she knew what happened, where she was, the seal-snake—the *eel*—seized the scissors and plunged them into her neck.

Eels are stronger than they look, but not strong enough.

The blades, large and blunt, banged against Mary's collarbone, sank into the soft skin, but not that far, and not in a dangerous place. Not dangerous for Mary, at least, but definitely dangerous for the eel.

Mary, who had never missed a day's workout even with all the mania of her new responsibilities, seized the eel and the scissors in her powerful grasp and pulled them away from her body. The scissors clattered onto the hardwood floor. Mary slammed the eel down on the floor beside them, driving her knee deep into the eel's soft, concave belly. Gasping against the pain, ignoring the blood that dripped heavily down into the eel's face, Mary bore down hard on the creature's wrists and spat in the terror-filled eyes.

Realizing after a moment that the eel couldn't breathe, Mary's own weight suffocating the pathetically weak beast, she relented, dragging the creature back up, up into the chair, baring its neck as she forced the head back into the sink where she had shampooed it. Raw fear constricted every vessel, every cell in the animal's face. Mary scooped up the scissors with her right hand as her left held the forehead in place. She despised the blood oozing from her own throat, preferring to leave it than to coddle herself. She stood there with the jagged, bloodied blades in her hand, waiting till the eel receded and the seal crept back into the wide, frightened eyes.

She hacked. She hacked and hewed and chopped.

By the time she was done, her breath wrenched her chest up and down, her blood pounding painfully against her veins.

The seal's face, bereft of its silken frame, ran wet with tears. The little face, so beloved, was contorted in an awful expression of agony and anticipation. Mary stroked the cheeks, ran the closed blade of the scissors along the trembling lips.

Another harsh lesson. How she hated these. The seal pup looked ridiculous and ashamed, her shorn scalp an open admission of guilt and remorse. Feeling impossibly old and impossibly heavy, Mary left the seal pup lying there, a huddled, shaking mass, and dragged herself to her pack. She withdrew the silken scarf she'd hoped to leave with the pup and tied a wide knot before wrapping it around her throat. There wasn't much bleeding left, but she didn't want an infection.

All she wanted to do was curl into a heap by the fire on the floor, but she knew the pup needed her now more than ever. Gently she drew the pup into a sitting position, pulled clean, soft pajamas over the chilled and shocky flesh. She stroked the bald little bony head and whispered nonsense into the pup's ears, cradling her against her body as she helped her climb into the warm, downy bed.

She sang Christmas carols until the pup's breathing eased. At last, they both slept, wrapped in each other's arms.

Spring would bring healing, and healing would bring happiness. Happiness for them both.

YEAR TWO
Noni Begay

It was hard to think through the pain, but harder still to sleep through it. Huddled naked under piles of blankets, Noni simultaneously dreaded and pined for the Mary-monster's return. When that engine sounded and Mary's steady tread approached, Noni's body hummed with terror and longing like discordant battling violins. Mary's return meant all good things: she would stoke the fire till the whole cabin thrummed with warmth and false solace, and Noni's aching muscles could finally ease the shivering that sent agony spiraling ceaselessly through her shattered bones. There'd be hot, delicious food, gentle sponge baths, and lit candles would disperse the heavy odors of sweat and fear and pain and excrement with cinnamon and teakwood. It was a lie. Noni knew all hope and comfort was a lie, but it was a lie she could not help yearning to be told.

The first few weeks were hellish. The slightest movement sent blinding anguish rattling through her veins, so she simply lay aching and freezing in her own filth under the blankets until Mary returned to clean her up. The older woman was coming more often now, though Noni's perception of day and night and the passage of time was muddy at best. In the days of solitude, Noni swore to herself that she would no longer plead with the Mary-monster, that she'd keep her words locked up tight behind her lips and save them for ears that would hear, like the stuffed rabbit tucked under the blankets with her or the Beaver Woman whose grain-carved face regarded her somberly from the chinked logs beside her bed.

But when Mary came through that door, shaking rain and snow from her hat and carrying sacks full of food and treats, words spilled unbidden from Noni's mouth like seawater through a dike. She hardly conceived their meaning herself, and they found no answering glint of comprehension in Mary's dull eyes, but she could not still them. They simply burbled, and Mary disregarded them as easily as she might have disregarded the furious scolding of a squirrel.

Caramels had been Noni's secret indulgence back in her former life, ruthlessly rationed out to herself a bite at a time on the campaign trail. Back then she'd been obsessed with her own image, managing every lock of hair and ounce of weight like a marketing ploy. She'd have long debates over the wisdom of feather earrings over pearls or square heels versus low-slung boots, certain that someone out there would base their vote on her choice. No doubt some had, and maybe if she'd been more principled, she wouldn't have cared. Maybe she'd have insisted that she only earn votes based on her platform and her goals and despised the rest. But what she'd wanted, more than anything, was a chance. A chance for herself to make a difference. A chance for the lost and discounted indigenous women across the continent to make their voices heard, their names remembered. A chance to transform the country. For that chance, she had no qualms about weaponizing her cheekbones and hemlines, if she must, for a seat at the table.

And damn them all. It had actually worked. She'd won her chance, a chance for all of them. And now it had been stolen away again, by the last person she'd have ever doubted. By the very person who'd fought tooth and nail alongside her to seize that opportunity. Noni still had no idea what Mary wanted. Maybe on the cusp of relinquishing Noni to Washington and national service, she'd simply cracked and decided to keep her surrogate daughter all to herself. That didn't make any sense—as long as Noni had known her, Mary's sole fuel had been her drive to find her daughter Ryska. Surely she wouldn't undermine those efforts for the chance to keep Noni close. But what else could explain what was happening?

For a while, Noni was wracked with the effort to understand her predicament, but she'd abandoned that. It didn't matter anymore why this was happening. It didn't matter what Mary wanted. All that mattered was surviving long enough to get away.

But in moments like this, with the warmth from the fire finally sinking all the way into her aching bones and sweet salted caramel melting like butter on her tongue, Noni struggled to remember that. Struggled even to remember her name. It had been so long since anyone had said it aloud. Without so much as a mirror in the cabin, she could almost doubt that she existed. Pain insisted she was here, but was she a being apart from pain? Or was she only agony itself, maybe even Mary's own agony over Ryska's absence made corporeal, a sort of sacrifice of spirit continually offered in this loneliest of places?

She swallowed the caramel, drank the sweet black coffee Mary had doctored for her, and gingerly unwrapped another caramel. She turned her head back to Beaver Woman's woodgrain face that watched her from the wall over her bed and silently asked her if she still had a face, still had a name.

Beaver Woman said she did.

Noni tried to believe her, but it was harder when Mary was there.

She sucked on another caramel. *Noni Begay loves caramels.*

Eventually Mary's visits became less frequent again, just as the weather turned back to the dreary chill of autumn. She left wood stacked just outside the cabin door, left a bit of bread and cold broth where Noni could reach them with enough effort. Noni's bones were finally knitting, but the pain, though less all-consuming, remained constant.

She quickly learned the importance of dragging in new wood before the fire went out completely. Just easing herself from the bed to the floor without jarring her legs took forever. At that point, the shivering inevitably set in, as Mary still wouldn't give her back her clothes. Arm over arm she would drag herself to the front door, screaming and crying as her legs jostled over the rug-covered wood floor. Then she'd sit in the open doorway as the wind whistled and cut its teeth on her bare flesh, throwing in as many logs as she could before the cold became too much to bear. After the first time, she thought to throw one of the blankets to the door first, so she could at least use its paltry warmth to shield herself from the worst of the gusts. Still, every time, the task was as exhausting in its relentless pain as in the energy it required.

Her blackest moment came not at the hands of pain or silence, but of time. She could no longer see more than sky out the window from her place on the bed, but the rapidly encroaching darkness and dropping temperatures forced her to acknowledge that an entire year must have passed. How was it possible that in all that time, no one had found her, no one had come to save her?

She knew how, though. Alaska was first and last an eater. Devourer of the dead and the living alike, it swallowed up anything that stood still in its murky mouth, covered the bones with moss and mushroom, curtained any trace of the trail with rampant wild roses, lurching trees, ravenous fireweed, and ankle-tan-gling ferns. Mere minutes from electric lights and paved roads, mountains and muskeg loomed forbidding, hostile and contemptuous of any inroads. Men pretending at survivalism might fly in, ride around, and fly out with their guns and bows, but only the unwary walked near enough to the earth here to hear its voice. A constant growl of magma and breaking stones, it told only of the pride of men, the power of old gods. It never whispered of escape.

How many women had waited to be found, to be saved? How many girls had watched the darkness come and go until it only came and stayed? How many bones fed the wildflower meadows? And on those paved roads, in those brightly lit houses and restaurants and stores, how many people still said their names, remembered their faces? How many badges still knocked on doors in their pursuit?

Short of a Hollywood celebrity or music star, Noni was as high-profile as a woman could get, and she could hardly remember her own name. It was too much to believe that anyone else remembered. Her parents, she knew. Izak, probably, though she'd tried to keep her erstwhile boyfriend at arms' length, just out of sight of cameras. All her friends were really acquaintances, carefully curated power brokers who might help her get one step closer to Washington. And she better than anyone knew how rare it was for the media and law enforcement to devote more than cursory time to yet another missing Native woman. Her status would have merited her a little extra attention, maybe even a handful of national headlines, but by now there'd be nothing to gain by throwing away airtime on her name. Alaska might as well be another country. Most Americans still called them Eskimos and probably thought they rode to school on polar bears.

Even so, giving up wasn't an option, though she'd caught herself wandering increasingly. Not physically, of course—months later, she could still barely put any weight on her legs. At night especially, she was still wracked with aching pain. But Noni wouldn't allow herself, even now, the luxury of a rescue fantasy. She'd always been too pragmatic to play the princess in a tower, even as a little girl. Rapunzel in particular had troubled her. If Rapunzel could make a ladder of her hair to allow the prince to clamber up, why hadn't she used the same method to let herself down long before he showed up?

So Noni tried hard to keep thoughts of her parents and Izak and even law enforcement at bay. She told her secrets to the stuffed bunny that lay beside her and the Beaver Woman who watched all things stolidly from her place in the log wall. Despite her best efforts to keep herself pinned to the sheets, she still caught herself adrift in stories she hadn't told, dream-laden with her eyes open, out in the cloud-draped sky. It was a bad sign, she knew, but it happened more and more often, and it was getting harder to refuse herself those few moments of peace and freedom.

She focused as much as she could on her way out. The first few weeks after the Mary-monster had broken her legs, she hadn't possessed the clarity of mind to think deliberately about anything, but now she returned to her old ploy—win the monster's trust. Again.

The last time she had relied on luck, on chance, and found that neither were on her side. More fool her. This time she would take a more direct approach. She couldn't afford to simply hope she'd manage to escape unnoticed and from there find a way back to civilization. She'd have to attack and disable Mary directly and use her transportation to follow the track back to the road.

For that she needed strength. Since she'd first met Mary, the woman had been devoted to her strength-training workouts at the gym. She wasn't a large woman, but she was built like a brickhouse. And even if she used every possible advantage and somehow overcame Mary, she still had to be strong enough to drive the All-Terrain Vehicle back to wherever Mary had parked her car. She had no way of knowing how far away that was, and controlling one of those machines over rough land was no small feat.

There wasn't anything she could do about her wasting, crooked legs, but Noni strengthened her upper body as best she could. It was hard to find exercises that wouldn't put pressure on her knitting bones. Lifts and push-ups were out of the question. She made barbells of tin cans filled with rocks. It wasn't much, but her muscles weren't much by now either. Still, little by little, her strength grew.

She waited, and she watched. She'd have exactly one moment, she knew. One chance to strike, when opportunity came. She asked Beaver Woman to stand close by, to help her transformation when the hour arrived.

It was a challenge to keep the gleam from her eyes, to hold her humble, mute expression when Mary offered to cut her hair. The sight of the gleaming shears in Mary's hand set Noni's belly trembling with want. Cold chills rushed over her body, driving out every other sensation, every other tendril of comprehension. All she saw—all she knew—was the blade.

After all those weeks of planning and waiting, there'd been no conscious decision, no hesitation. Noni simply unwound all her being into seizing and wielding those scissors, sighing the sweetest pleasure into her exhale as she felt the steel find its home in Mary's neck.

But something went horribly wrong. Triumph lasted less than a second.

Maybe Mary really was a monster. Maybe she couldn't be killed. Maybe there was no way out. Maybe this was all there was.

Before she knew what happened, Noni was back under restraint, her fleeting breath of freedom extinguished in the bitter ash of despair. She bucked and howled as terror fought its way free of her lungs and limbs, leaving only hopelessness in its wake. Mary grasped hanks of Noni's hair, chopped them ruthlessly away with the blood-stained shears till nothing remained on her skull but coarsely broken tufts. The older woman breathed heavily, her blood dripping onto Noni's body as she plied her task. The scents of blood and sweat mingled with the cinnamon candles still burning in a macabre imitation of a Christmas celebration.

Noni went wandering after that.

She followed Beaver Woman out past the meadow, deep into the trees. A wide river whose name she didn't know curled there, continually shaking itself free of the grasping roots of the spruce and alders along its banks.

Noni Begay would have wondered why the waters still ran free, unslurried by ice. Noni Begay would have wondered why the crimson salmon leapt wide-eyed from the river so late in the year. Noni Begay would have wondered where came this sun whose healing light sank deep in her aching bones and lifted her, step by step, to the beaver dam clambering cathedral-like out of the water.

But Noni Begay was only a name given to a body whose broken pieces served no purpose. She was a ghost, a spirit, the drab smudge left behind by a broken pencil. She trailed behind Beaver Woman, and behind her trailed the ghost of a rabbit. The rabbit ghost looked like the stuffed bunny the Mary-monster had given her, but Noni knew she was all that remained of Ryska. Mary thought Ryska was still alive out there somewhere, waiting for her mother to find her, but here she was, wandering with Noni.

Noni crouched, settling herself onto a wide log. Rabbit snuffled at the crushed wildflowers and set to nibbling, her dark liquid eyes untroubled. Rabbit's fight was over. She no longer sought escape. Rabbit hopped through these woods and meadows with no fear of eagles or hawks or coyotes. Here winter was not coming. Here the predators did not win.

Beaver Woman gestured to the salmon.

Noni lost herself in the patterned flash of golden sunlight on scarlet scales, dropping uncounted into blue river that might too be blue sky. She no longer felt the branches of the dam under her thighs, no longer tasted air. She only leapt and flashed and swam, eternally bound for the nethers, eternally traveling, eternally submitting and eternally saving herself.

Rabbit sat solemn in the sun.

But even eternity must fade into measured hours. Beaver Woman tugged her free of the river, lifted her from the dam, set her feet back on the path through the woods to the cabin. The old panic did not rise. She did not resist the pull back to time, to walls, to a dying fire and a cold bed. It wasn't real, after all. It would cost her nothing to sleep, to dream a while and endure fantastic falsehoods for a few hours. Now she had the real to cling to, she was unassailable by poor pretended agonies.

Ice bit, fire leapt, Rabbit curled up in the blankets beside her while Beaver Woman hummed them softly to sleep.

Thunder was rare—here the gods whispered their threats—so when Noni heard the rumble, she knew the Mary-monster was back. She ran her fingers over her nearly bald scalp, her fingertips lingering on the bony ridges as she listened to the steps approaching. Beaver Woman had shown her how to defeat the wendigo. She must tame the darkened spirit, find some bright silver thread still among its rotten fabric that she might tie to herself.

It was easier than she expected, though she sometimes got confused about which way the thread was pulling. She adopted the manifestation of Rabbit, accepting with soft mouth every morsel of food or kindness. For every pleasure given—warmth or meat or sugar or the almost unbearable sweetness of Mary's strong hands easing the aches of the tangled muscles in her twisted legs—Noni offered a pleasure of her own, tucking her head into the curve of Mary's shoulder, clutching her hand. Rabbit watched, still-faced, no longer craving domestication and alone in her untethering.

Noni learned to drift between joys. While the Mary-monster was there, their shared parody of familial love nearly fooled her too. Mary would build a blazing fire and fill the tiny cabin with fragrances of delicious food and decadent candles. She and Noni and Rabbit would curl up together at night under heaps of soft blankets and watch the stars spin through the window. Mary would pet her head and file her fingernails and brush her teeth.

And when the Mary-monster left…when she left, Noni would return to the real world. Leaving the paper-doll walls of the cabin behind, she and Rabbit and Beaver Woman roamed the hills, swam the rivers, fell into the skies. She ate the flesh of the salmon and learned their stories, she followed the owl and fought laughing with the ermine.

Never again, she swore to Rabbit. Never again would she believe the lies. She had stripped her eyes of their dross. Now she would only accept the real. Here, in the arms of the sun, beneath the gaze of the moon, she would stay. Paper walls could burn.

YEAR THREE
Mary Nelson

Mary kept a shotgun slung across her broad shoulders and a can of bear spray hanging from a carabiner on her backpack as she rumbled across the mostly frozen muskeg toward the cabin where her seal pup waited, but she wasn't afraid of bears. Bears were powerful, wise spirit beings with purposes of their own that generally had no truck with people. Still, if she got in the way of that purpose, she was prepared to defend her life. And sometimes even a bear's spirit got twisted up. Everyone knew someone who'd been stalked, hunted across the wilderness by a bear who had forgotten it was a bear.

Mary hunched her shoulders against the cold and tried not to let her teeth bang as she bumped and rattled along the uneven ground. Folks liked to tell stories of werewolves and ice cannibals, but Mary knew they had it all wrong. The spirit of the animal could only make a man better. The truly terrifying evil that walked this earth was entirely and utterly human. Nothing shone in its eyes but the hunger of its flesh—no spirit, no sky. No beast.

The irony of keeping her seal pup locked away out here while all the world looked for her was that this was the only place she could be safe. The cormorants imagined that they would be rescuing her if they found her, but they'd only be returning to her to the constant peril in which pups like her and rabbits like Ryska walked every day. It didn't do, she knew, to compare one woman's experience with another's, but sometimes she couldn't help it.

Her lips curled. The so-called "Me Too" movement of a few years back had fizzled out quickly. Calling out sexual assault had provided a brief sensational feeding for the coyotes, a few men had been fired, a few women had gotten famous, and then life returned to typical aside from a few extra sessions of harassment training scheduled by HR departments every year. Mary didn't want to despise all the white women who wore their sexual assault badges with honor or tried to outdo each other with the subtlety of their experience—*oh, sure, you had to wear dresses to the office but did I tell you about the time I regretted having sex with a man who enjoyed it more than me*—but she did despise them all the same.

She'd have loved the luxury of recounting dirty jokes as an example of how women were treated in her experience. She'd have loved to complain about female cops not being allowed to wear fingernail polish or about women in entertainment being expected to stay skinny and keep their skin smooth. Imagine, she thought bitterly, her lip twisting, if the man who most hurt and enraged you as a woman lived thousands of miles away in a white house in a big city and had no idea who you were.

She didn't give a shit about fingernail polish or hemlines or cleavage. She got the argument that it was a symptom of the same problem, but then attack the damn problem instead of chasing down every stray symptom as if every one were a violation of the Geneva Convention. Did it suck to have to make men feel important and bring them coffee and smile when they smiled? Of course it sucked, but it was hardly traumatic. Mary knew trauma. She knew the flavor it left in your mouth, the tremors it left deep in your veins that never stopped vibrating, the way it twisted bones and twisted minds.

Her little seal pup wasn't sacrificing her freedom so that women could have an easier time in the office or at the grocery store. This was about life and death.

How many hundreds of Native women and little girls had been missing and murdered, just in the last ten years since Ryska was taken? Back when she and the pup had been working on the campaign, they'd done all kinds of research, talked to all kinds of experts, but it had proved hardly worth the effort. Where communities and law enforcement agencies did keep records, the numbers were staggering, but most communities and agencies didn't track the Native missing at all. Lumping them in with everyone else camouflaged the horror. Even at the federal level, information was scant and hard to come by. What little they found was terrifying enough: Native women were being kidnapped and murdered at rates that confounded comprehension. Thousands more were reported at local levels than ever made it into national databases, so God only knew how bad it really was. The one statistic Mary did know, impossible to forget, was that Native women were ten times more like to die by murder than a woman of any other ethnicity.

And somehow, that wasn't even the most horrifying aspect of the facts. What was worse was that Native women were overwhelmingly, almost exclusively, being murdered by white men.

And that brought her back to fingernail polish. It wasn't about all the hundreds of micro-accommodations that women made for men on a daily basis without even noticing. It was about the root concept that women existed to serve, protect, and defend men, that they had no value beyond what they could offer to a man. Somehow, that belief was magnified a hundredfold when it came to white men and Native women.

Her little seal pup had been passionate about uncovering that fat albino anaconda that lurked under the rocks and leaves of American society, and Alaskan society in particular. She'd truly believed that she could drag its immense grotesque body out into the sun and leave it there to wither and die. She hadn't understood than even politicians in Washington were little more than distractions, propped-up cut-outs with scrolling subtitles paraded in front of cameras so that the real powers—intelligence, communications, financial, administrative, bureaucratic—could continue to consolidate power and trade funds without attracting any attention. The fate of a few hundred or even a few thousand Native women would not provide more than a moment's entertainment as far as they were concerned. The pup would have been patted on the head, handed a few thousand dollars, given a committee or two, and then would have been soundly ignored from there.

Oh, Mary supposed she might have been able to get an extra chapter or two of Native education added to state-approved textbooks. She might have been able to institute better tracking practices among law enforcement agencies. But give her the voice and platform to reach into men's souls, to change hearts, to stir up fury and outrage?

To find the girls?

Mary shook her head as she dismounted, dislodging the damp snow that had settled on her shoulders as she'd made her way to the cabin. Not hardly. The missing and the dead had no monetary value, and their only political value was as the lost. Found broken girls and unburied bodies were of no use to anyone.

Boarded up, moss-eaten, and sagging, the cabin would have looked completely abandoned if not for the cozy curl of grey smoke wisping up toward the greyer sky. The boards crisscrossed over the front door were only subterfuge, though, and Mary entered easily. The pup met her at the door, laughing as she helped unwrap Mary almost as if she were a toilet paper mummy, removing hat and scarf, gloves and coat, boots and backpack and saddlebags. After a quick, cursory hug, the pup scampered to the table with the gear in her arms, eager to dig through the packs' contents.

Mary settled into the wooden rocking chair near the fireplace, leaning forward with her elbows on her thick thighs as she warmed her hands. She didn't like to watch the pup as she happily tore into her new treats.

Last year had been…hard, Mary concluded, with customary understatement.

She reached into the thigh pocket of her cargo pants and withdrew her flask, taking a healthy swallow before tucking it back away. She didn't like to think back on how her seal pup had suffered, although she had no doubt that it had been even harder on her. After all, she was the one in control, the one who had to make the hard decisions. There was some comfort in helplessness, she believed. Some solace in reliance.

But for Mary, there had been no comfort, no solace. She'd had to face up to the hard decisions and hold to them, no matter what. Back at home, in the drawer of her nightstand, she still had a long, beautiful, silken lock of the seal pup's hair. She carefully braided and beaded it, kept it beside the scrap of Ryska's baby blanket and her little jar of baby teeth. Even now, the pup's lovely fur was little more than a cap, barely chin-length. Mary had taken care of it, though, trimmed it up as it grew, so it gleamed in the firelight. Every time she looked at her, even now, she fought not to wince.

It wasn't just the hair. It was the pup's eyes, too. No longer angry and resentful or beaten and afraid, instead they followed her continually with doting care, warm and gently anxious, more like a hound pup than a seal pup.

Mary supposed she should be grateful. The pup was definitely much easier to handle. Mary no longer feared escape attempts and was able to give the pup much more freedom, which amounted to more comforts. She still kept supplies short, and travel for the pup was virtually impossible, but at least she could care for herself while Mary was away. No more coming back to filth and having to bathe the pup on every trip. No more ropes and worries about blood clots and atrophy.

Against her will, Mary's eyes slid to watch the pup hobbling around the table with glee, the small dark head and tiny fingers bobbing in and out of the bags, punctuated by little exclamations of delight. She sucked in her lips, returned her gaze to the fire.

Easier was rarely better. She'd hammered her pup with that concept when they'd been campaigning. Together they'd focused on the hard targets. Naturally they'd still scooped up the easy ones on the way in—no politician left votes on the ground—but their goal had always been the pinnacle, not the false summits. They hadn't aimed for the Native men who thought she was pretty—they went after the grandmothers who hadn't voted in decades or maybe never at all. They'd campaigned on a fierce demand that environmental groups and the oil companies work together, not just continually lob accusations at each other and stay permanently on opposite sides of the table. They'd vowed a hard line on crime but insisted on taxes to improve mental health facilities.

Who knows if they'd ever have been able to deliver on any of it? Just getting voters to back it had been magical enough.

This hungry, sweet little seal pup who tucked her head under Mary's arm and nuzzled at her cheeks was a stranger. Mary missed her warrior-daughter, her wild Noni.

But the seal pup was going to save her Ryska. Mary mustn't forget that. She had to hold fast to her course however the wind blew and the seas swelled. Her baby's bones called out for her.

Mama. Mama, I'm so scared. Mama, please help me. Please. Mama.

It would be okay, wouldn't it? Okay if the pup had lost all its feral instincts?

She tried not to flinch when the pup curled up at her feet in front of the fire, wrapping one arm around Mary's stout, strong calf and happily munching a deli sandwich with the other.

Mary had never been an *ends justify the means* kind of person. Things were good or evil in and of themselves, as far as she was concerned, even if that meant choosing the harder path. The seal pup had done the hard good thing by sacrificing herself to help find Ryska. Maybe Mary needed to do the hard good thing and help the pup find herself again.

Reluctantly she rested her hand on the pup's sleek head, every silken bump and knob familiar.

The pup was paying a high price, and still Mary was no nearer to finding her daughter than she had been when this all began. Not for lack of trying. Mary's left hand crept up to the gold crucifix that hung around her neck. The Great Spirit had sacrificed his Son to save the world. She could sacrifice this pup to save her daughter. But what if she could save them both?

Mary had badly misjudged the interest of coyotes in the flavor of truth.

Rotten meat smelled many times more fragrant and drew more scavengers than truth ever could. But no new leads meant Ryska's story reeked only of old bones. Maybe if her boyfriend could have been interviewed, it would have excited more interest, but he was out on a rig somewhere, not due back by deadline. Even this year, on the third anniversary of the pup's disappearance, Ryska had barely merited a footnote. Just another of the many "missing and murdered indigenous women and girls."

#MMIWG

A trending hashtag, ironically, was a death knell. Now those girls were nothing more than a byline, a hip poster reference, another reason to paint the face and march the protest and generally take up a safe place where politicians and newscasters could poll you and trust you to stay there. Crying out in the name of a hashtag was about as revolutionary as piercing your nose or paying a guy $300 to paint *RESIST* on your bicep, up where you could cover it when you went to work. People felt like heroes because they shared your post on Facebook or liked your Tweet, and then they ordered a pizza and watched the game.

The pup was mewling, pushing her head against Mary's knee.

Mary struggled to her feet. Damn knees. She was so much older than her years. But slowing down was not an option now. She hung the big kettle of water over the stove and handed the pup the hygiene products she had brought. Soon the pup could take the bath she clearly craved. In the meantime, Mary would fix a real supper on the woodstove. The pup had already happily ordered the canned goods and boxed and bagged products on her meager shelves. They would last her comfortably about ten days. Mary would be back in fourteen, if not more. Hunger, craving, wanting, was an essential part of their relationship now.

Mashed potatoes and fried halibut. Mary always tried to make her hot meals one of the seal pup's favorites. Back on the campaign trail, it had been a constant balancing act. As a woman, the pup had needed to look pretty enough for the men to vote for, professional enough for the women to vote for, and "Alaska" enough for the newcomers to the state to vote for. Being seen in public eating traditional Alaskan fare—which had resulted in Alaska being one of the fattest states in the country—while still fitting into her slim slacks and pencil skirts had been a constant challenge. Now the pup could eat what she wanted. When it was available. There was still no danger of overindulgence, even with her severely restricted mobility since the incident with her legs. And constant positive sensory reinforcement had been vital to the pup's retraining after all the rebellion of last year and consequent punishments.

Mary set the seal pup's heaping platter on the floor near the fire and settled back into the rocking chair with a stifled groan. She couldn't help taking pleasure in the pup's blissful eating; she supposed that was a hard-wired genetic tendency in women. In mothers, at least, and likely as often in wives, though she wouldn't know that herself. Evolutionary brilliance. Ensure that females derived actual endorphins from feeding young, and the process takes care of itself.

For her own part, she merely forced the few bites she'd reserved to her own plate past her lips. She'd long since lost almost all sense of taste. It had worried her at first, but she was accustomed to it now. If she could have quit eating altogether, she would have. Even breathing exhausted her. But she had to feed the machine, had to keep going. For Ryska's sake, and for the pup, too.

After dinner, she retrieved from the table the small handmade book that the pup had discarded in her wild excavation of the saddlebags. A real Christmas present, more valuable by far than any store-bought trinket. Food was the single motivator for the pup these days, but Mary was determined to change that. Maybe it was dangerous, maybe she'd regret it, but she had to give the pup a chance to come back from the dark den into which she'd all but entirely retreated. Mary wanted to see something besides submission in those eyes.

Caution, she understood, was vital. But forcing the pup to lose all sense of self, to disappear entirely, was not an option for her. Mary had to find a way to paint her back in without allowing her to climb out of the frame. This book was one small stroke, one new color on the canvas.

Mary stroked the soft fabric cover with reverent hands. She'd paid an exorbitant price to have the book made. Only a handful of people remained who spoke the Aleut language, fewer yet who could write it. She'd met a grandmother painter at an art fair last year, in the midst of the worst of the pup's rebellion, and she'd asked the grandmother to make this book for her. It was a recounting of the story of the girl who married the moon. Grandmother Alice's paintings formed the canvas pages. The tale was told in hand-printed black *Unangam Tunuu*, quavery but clear.

Mary didn't speak or read *Unangam Tunuu* herself, naturally, and neither did the seal pup. But words, Mary knew, words have power. She'd kept that power from the pup for over two years now. Today, she would give it back.

Mary turned back the bedcovers and propped up the pillows. She slipped on her pajamas and motioned to the pup to join her as she climbed into the bed with the book in her hand. For the first time, the pup registered the object, and an indecipherable darkness moved in those vapid eyes. A little shiver of something like fear moved through Mary, but she pushed it aside. The pup retrieved the ragged stuffed rabbit that accompanied her everywhere and crawled up beside Mary.

Mary had expected the words to feel heavy in her mouth, jagged and unfamiliar, but the sounds rolled around like smooth stones in sea silt and saltwater, harmonic and hypnotic. The seal pup gasped at the sound of Mary's voice but immediately subsided, as if afraid that the words would stop if she acknowledged their receipt. Utterly rapt, the pup hardly glanced at the beautiful, color-drenched paintings, her gaze instead fixed on Mary's lips.

The flavor of these words was unfamiliar to Mary, but the story was not. As syllables dropped from her lips and her gaze filled with the images that the grandmother had painted, the story swelled within her. Her pronunciation was all wrong, and she could not have said which word meant moon or which word meant night. And still, she understood. She hoped the pup did, too.

Though from the earth, the moon seems changeable and fickle, he is a steady and constant being, faithful to his duties and devoted in his affections. The trouble is with what we see, not with who he is. So he is unaffected by the quarrels of lovers and the longings of silly young girls.

But two young cousins were different. They wanted to marry the moon, and every night, they would sit up on the beach to watch his journey, calling out his name and promising him their love. For a long time, he ignored their childish play, but years passed and their devotion remained unchanged. Finally, he came to the shore to meet them.

"I can only marry the most patient of you," he explained, but they both implored him. He wrapped their long hair around each of his hands.

"Close your eyes until we get to my home," he cautioned them. They felt themselves lifted away, soaring through the air.

One of the cousins soon became impatient at the long journey and opened her eyes. The stars fell away from her as she was drawn back, back, back down to the earth.

The other maiden made it all the way to the moon's home. It was a beautiful place, and they were very happy, consumed in each other's love when the moon was not working. But the moon often worked, and to the maiden his hours were long and strange. Sometimes he worked all night, sometimes in the morning, sometimes late in the afternoon. She grew restless and lonely, and she implored her husband to let her accompany him on his work.

"My work is too hard for you," he told her. "You cannot help me. But you may explore this place while I am away. Only do not look behind the curtains in the two houses you can see from our home. That is forbidden."

The moon's wife was glad to adventure on her own the next time the moon left her behind. She discovered the Star-People, men with one great glittering eye in the middle of their forehead who lay prone, gazing down at the world through holes in the ground. She played and explored, but the mystery of what lay behind the curtains in those two houses ate at her heart.

Finally, she gave in to her curiosity and went inside first one, then the other, drawing back the curtains. In each barabara, *or house, she found three moon-face masks: one for each of the phases of the moon. Admiring their beauty and light, she could not resist putting the mask of the nearly full moon on her own face. To her horror, she found she could not remove it.*

She ran home, weeping, and tried to hide her face in the blankets in bed. When the moon came home, he knew what she had done. But he was not angry.

"I could not ask you to share my hard work with me," he told her. "But you have taken it on of your own desire. Together we walk the paths of the moon now."

Now the moon and his wife share the long journeys across the sky and take turns with the work they have been given. Some nights the moon may look on us, and some nights his wife, but in love they are one.

◇◆◇◆◇

Mary closed the book as the final words filled the room, but the seal pup snatched at the pages, pawing them back open to the beginning. She did not speak, but only pleaded with Mary with her eyes, dark and wet and full of longing. So Mary read again.

She didn't think she needed to explain to the pup that they were like the moon and his wife. Back when she'd first met the seal pup, in those early years after Ryska was gone, she'd never dreamed of a wild plan like the one they were living now. But as the pup had grown into her role as a spokesperson not just for Alaska but specifically for Native women, she'd grown more and more passionate about the issue of missing and murdered indigenous women. Even in the Native villages, information could be scant. Even white women, Mary knew, worried about attacks so common as to be downright casual. She'd often wondered what it was like to be a man, to never worry about sleeping under an open window or walking to your car or leaving your drink or smiling too much, smiling not enough, smiling the wrong way.

Learning that native women were many times more likely to be kidnapped, many times more likely to be murdered, had been sobering enough. Learning that unlike in other demographics, where the violence was most often at the hands of someone who shared the same skin color as the victim, Native women were almost exclusively being hunted by white men was downright terrifying.

And for her little seal pup, that terror had fueled a beautiful, blazing rage. She'd been unstoppable. No matter what else she addressed at public gatherings, whether she was meeting oil execs or salmon fishers, the Sierra Club or the teachers' association, she brought up the issue. She made sure no one forgot.

Just like the moon's wife, she'd taken on this hard, hard work of her own volition. Mary could never have asked her to. But now…now they were in it together. Together they would bring Ryska home. Together they would say the names of all the missing girls till the stars shouted those names back at them.

FOUND.

The seal pup cried pitifully when Mary laid the book aside for the night and turned down the lamp. In the darkness, as the fire cracked and popped, Mary spooned her little pup, wrapping the pup's bony arms in her strong embrace and hugging the little ragged rabbit against them both. The day after tomorrow, when she returned to the land of coyotes and cormorants, she would take the book back with her, and she knew the pup would only cry even harder then. But for now, they could close their eyes and dream of the moon together.

And perhaps, somewhere out there under this same moon, a little rabbit danced on the grass, waiting for her mother.

YEAR THREE
Noni Begay

Noni sat on the edge of the forest clearing, her legs stretched out in front of her, soaking up the late evening sun that still floated high in the sky. A sort of darkness would drift sometime in the wee hours and drift out again before ever really taking hold. The sun would bob up again like a buoy escaping a weight and float back across the waves of sky. Summer days were harder to count than winter nights.

Blueberries burst tart on her tongue, staining her fingers and lips. Beside her lay a basket half-filled with bounty. She'd come out here with a purpose, but what was the point of purpose? The sun was warm, the berries delectable, the grass sweet. Sitting here while the trees murmured behind her, shaking out droplets of sunshine over her bare skin, was purpose enough.

She squinted at the sky. Were the Star-People watching her now, she wondered. Could they still see her through these long, long days, or was their vision blinded by the brash insistence of the sun? Panic rose in her throat like a bird trapped in a wall, and wretchedly she plucked its feathers and forced the flightless beast down into her belly. If the Star-People didn't see her, did anyone see her? Was she even here anymore? Had she become only an echo of her own name?

Her last fear, she clung to it as fiercely as she clung to Rabbit, who even now hunched raggedly beside her, a pile of berries between its paws. Pain had long since become a constant companion, a measure of breath and nothing more. Certainly nothing to be dreaded or even avoided. Nightmares had dogged her for a while, but once Beaver Woman had shown her the way out, their small threats had faded. The Mary-monster was Mary-mother, Mother Mary, now. The rumbling of her thunder feet only signaled pleasures and comforts.

Sweetest of all the pleasures was the sylvan waterfall of words she brought with her. Noni's world had been silent so long, the music that ordered her thoughts fell into tuneless chaos. For a while, she tried talking to herself, to hold ideas to words and words to a rhythm that created melody, but those words ran up and down the scale and out of reach. Next, she scratched messages to herself with sticks in the dirt, but the rain washed them all away. Growing resentful of their rebellion, she let them go, only occasionally harnessing them to her musings.

When Mary-mother had brought The Book, all Noni's music came rushing back, snatching every wandering note out of the air into a symphony of song. It didn't matter that the sounds were unfamiliar, unhitched to any lullaby she knew. That ragged rhythm spilling from Mary-mother's mouth summoned an automatic answer from Noni's throat, versicle and response holier than any Mass.

It had been Christmas, but the trappings of the custom fell away from Noni's perception and all she saw, all she heard, all she knew was language. At her soundless pleading, Mary-mother had read the story again and again, till her voice fell harsh and soft in Noni's ears. When Mary-mother left, she took the precious Book with her. Although Noni had watched her pack the treasure away in her pack before she mounted the ATV and roared away, she couldn't help searching for it all the same. She looked behind every can of food, scrabbled at the back of every drawer, as if it might retake a corporeal form there by some magic of its own. However she hunted, the words were gone, the story silent.

So Noni had practiced a sort of necromancy, calling back the spirit of the pages and forcing it to take a form her spirit could see. She spent long hours perfectly still, her eyes closed, but her mind open, recounting sound by sound the story only her heart knew. She summoned up the heavy black strokes of ink she had traced while Mary read over her shoulder and recited to herself their shapes. After so many months of silence, it hadn't been easy to coax tamed words out of her own throat, fit their edges to the lines she'd memorized, but she tried again and again until the stammers changed to symphonies.

She didn't need to understand the form of the words to know the story told on the brilliantly painted pages. It was her own story. Although she'd never met Ryska, she knew instinctively Ryska was the girl who had been taken to the sky, and Noni was the one who had fallen back to earth. Like her, Ryska had bided her time and lulled her captor into a false sense of security before robbing him of his light so she could share it freely with those still wandering below. Ryska was the Rabbit in the moon, shepherdess of the Star-People who watched over Noni and all the other lost girls, sent their silvery light piercing through the night to illuminate the path out.

That had been solace enough in the deep grey of winter days and the obsidian nights, but in the bleak and constant light of summer, Noni feared the Star-People had lost sight of her. She had lost sight of them. Now that the bushes were heavy with berries, the sun bobbed farther and farther away. She only hoped as autumn put on her dancing dress, the Star-People would find her again and mark her steps. If they forgot her, who would remember? Her name sounded unfamiliar in her own mouth, rolling around behind her teeth like a river rock.

Still, she bit determinedly into its hard surface, determined to keep it as her own. As she imagined turning the pages of her precious treasure, chanting its words aloud, she added her own name to the end of every sentence, as if she might incant herself to keep her being whole.

She pushed herself to her feet, tucking Rabbit into her berry basket and hobbling back to the cabin with her new rolling gait. She didn't think she'd ever walk straight again. Running seemed an impossibility. But every step was affirmation of her own strength and will, every step its own discrete victory. She was more than the amalgamation of her hurts and griefs.

Her basket was barely half-full, but she knew only one thing would keep her wounded panic well at bay. What began as consolation had rapidly become compulsion. She closed the cabin door behind her against the mosquitoes and shrews and propped Rabbit with her nose against the glass so she wouldn't feel too claustrophobic. She walked to the little shelf beside the wood stove where a blank space stood well-dusted and conspicuously empty.

She drew from the air and sat down in her little chair, turning pages that weren't there as she read to herself from the specter of The Book. As long as The Book *was*, somewhere, anywhere, she could reach it. Could read it. Could find herself on its colorful pages, starkly real in its black ink.

Noni, she fairly shouted at the end of every sentence. *Noni*.

Marrying her name to the strange words somehow married her existence to the living spirits of the people who knew those words. If her name could still find a space among strangers, she could too.

Noni. Noni. Noni Begay.

By the time she came to the last page, her heartbeat had eased its frantic pace. Her breath came slow and regular. Sun no longer seemed such a hostile companion. Birdsong and leaf-chatter drifted around the corners of the log walls. Her spirit had stopped tugging on her sinews, restless and dissatisfied with its restraints. Beaver Woman sat cross-legged on the floor opposite, her back leaned against the wall of the cabin below the window. She did not speak—even now, Beaver Woman did not dull her tongue with speech—but she smiled at Noni as if she, too, found peace in the recitation of her name.

Sometimes Noni got confused about which way the tether was supposed to pull. She had been so sure, for a while, that the cabin walls were only paper after all, that when she closed her eyes and stopped believing, they simply curled into ash and disappeared. That the bodies of her brother salmon slipping and sliding over her bare flesh, the fists of the mother mountains breaking boulders into sandcastles, the talons of the shaman owls tearing her old rotten skin away and leaving her clean and new, were all the real. The Book had fuddled that.

The Book was definitely real. Her name, spoken in its voice, was real. But The Book belonged here, in the paper world. So what did that say about her? Was she only real here too, in the paper world? Beaver Woman walked between both worlds without any sign of distress or confusion. Maybe that was all Noni needed to do. Maybe there wasn't one real world and one paper world. Maybe both were real.

Maybe both were paper.

A flutter in her throat. Noni shook her head, pushed the thought away. *I'm real,* she told herself silently. *I'm real, I'm real, I'm real.*

At first she had tried building a library of her own. Walking the uneven ground, with its swampy pools, stubborn outcroppings of weeds, tangled underbrush, and hidden deadfalls, was a painful and laborious process, so she still didn't venture too far beyond the trees ringing her small clearing. But a few yards into the moss-curtained, sunlight-dappled forest, where she could hear the inhaling and exhaling of the earth, she had built a bookshelf of broken limbs, a reading nook cushioned with ferns and rotting bark. But try as she might, she couldn't conjure any titles for her shelves.

It wasn't as if she hadn't been a reader back in her former life. Her mind snagged on that idea, distracted. Former life. That was right, wasn't it? She'd had a different life, been a different person once, hadn't she? Or was that only a dream?

It hardly seemed reasonable now, to think that she might have measured her days and her worth by the number of meetings she attended and the earrings she wore and the hands she shook. Everything then had felt so urgent, so necessary, so vital. Now nothing was urgent. She would be hungry until she was filled, she would be still till she moved, she would dream till she woke. She was never alone—Rabbit and Beaver Woman walked everywhere with her, and they brought her effortlessly into communion with all they encountered. Noni could feel the laughter of the birches and taste the triumph of the salmon, she could find snow abeyant in a sun-warmed wind and hear the rivers of fire rumbling under the earth. What could be more real than this?

She stared, nonplussed, at the empty shelves standing on the forest floor. Books belonged there. Her mind refused to give that up, but still, no books would come. She squeezed her eyes tightly closed and fought to picture a book, any book, but the images were indistinct, immaterial. She tried to focus on the titles, but the ink blurred and wriggled away, earthworms slithering into a muddy bank ahead of a river rushing in flood. The only story she could remember now was the story of Ryska and Noni and the Star-People.

Forlornly she stocked her poor library with pinecones and quartz rocks, placeholders for books she hoped might arrive later. The library became part of her regular track. She visited there most days, when rain and wind didn't keep her cabin bound. She sorted and ordered, sorted and ordered, her tiny collection, replacing titles as they were stolen by squirrels or greedy ravens. As the light began to withdraw more and more into itself, trailing the long grey locks of her hair across the forest floor, Noni had to clear away fallen leaves and broken limbs to keep the shelves clear. She built a wall of rocks to protect her curation from wind and rain and what she knew would soon be the advent of snow.

Beaver Woman, she knew, did not approve. Beaver Woman wanted her to leave the paper world inside of the paper walls, and books and libraries belonged to the paper world. Noni wasn't sure what prompted her rebellion. She trusted Beaver Woman. Beaver Woman did not hurt her or lie to her. Beaver Woman had shown her the path to transformation, taught her to swim with salmon and fly with the eagles and run with the wolves. Beaver Woman was not afraid of the long nights or wearied by the long days.

Still, whatever kept her from yielding entirely to Mary-mother kept her from Beaver Woman, too. Mary-mother wanted to believe, though, and so Noni's small insularity escaped her notice. Beaver Woman did not want, did not need—she simply *was*, and she regarded Noni's refusal to consent without caveat to truth with wide eyes. Noni could not lie to her.

Unlike Mary-mother, Mary-monster, Beaver Woman did not punish Noni for her revolt. Noni was not her captive, merely her companion. While Beaver Woman found Noni's insistence on this pitiful parody of the paper world out here in the world of earth and sea and sky absurd, she permitted it.

Every time Mary-mother returned, she brought The Book with her. Noni's former glee over fried halibut and salted caramels was soundly displaced by its arrival. However irrational, a quiet terror of Mary forgetting the sacred object or, worse, withholding it out of some cruel impulse, ran quivering through Noni's veins from the moment her ears picked up the rumble of the ATV until she retrieved The Book from Mary's pile of bags and boxes. Sweet relief swamped her senses with its hot pleasure, left her incoherent as her fingers found their old paths along the heavily-drawn ink.

Delight quickly gave way to gratitude, and she wrapped her arms tightly around Mary's stout figure. Comfort and consolation spread through her bones like warmth as Mary hugged her back and stroked the silky hair that still lay close to her scalp, barely extending past her ears.

Mary only stayed two or three days at a time, but these oases became the focus of Noni's existence. In the space between visits, Noni looked back on her time with Mary as a kind of song suspended, like the music that fell from the curtains of the aurora borealis or the symphonies of whales out in the sound. The details blurred and faded, but she remembered the notes rising and falling, striking deep in her bones and drifting out, away, aloft among the clouds. She craved the song more than she craved food or water or sunlight, and for the first day or two after Mary and The Book were gone, she would sink into an unremitting blackness, her ears aching with silence.

Beaver Woman and Rabbit would wait patiently by her side, stroking her arms and breathing sweet fragrant promises in her face until she rose at last. They would coax her back out into the waiting light, remind her of all that was real. Still the song would linger along the edges of her mind, sometimes picking up a new rhythm in the ruffling of fireweed in the wind, the rustling of lost leaves, the rattling of river stones. She was a ship with two anchors, and she did not know which lay in the rocks and which in the sea.

And when the crescendo rose, when Mary stepped back into the cabin as the whole earth swelled in song, Noni didn't even care. She only wanted to hear one more note.

At night, Noni lay tucked against Mary's shoulder as she read. When the words subsided into Mary's rattling snores, Noni curled her back against Mary-mother's warm body, pulled Rabbit close under the covers. She lay in the darkness, staring into Beaver Woman's wood-carved eyes until dreams tugged her loose.

High above the earth, the Star-People kept their gaze on all the lost children as they wandered. They did not look on the wendigo, did not acknowledge its name.

YEAR FOUR
Mary Nelson

Damn ravens with their shiny eyes, dark doors that opened on nothing. Mary knew that her distaste was a consequence of her own growth and no fault of their own, but still she despised them. Once they'd been comrades; once she'd actually taken pride in how well they'd worked together. After all, ravens were death-eaters, scavengers of life; they ingested wisdom and saw what stood on both sides of a man's breath. Fellow dreamers, she'd thought them, builders and purveyors of a future that most people wouldn't even fathom, much less craft. Above all, most excellent of storytellers.

Oh, Mary knew the popular disdain the average person held for politicians, but she'd always considered that the natural resentment of the sheep for the shepherd. It was all well and good to sit in the home someone else had provided for you, enjoy the freedoms someone else had died for, and comfortably criticize every effort to change and improve things. The percentage of people who couldn't even be troubled to vote was staggering. The number of people who did more than just fill in a tick box, people who actually recognized problems, considered solutions, and acted to implement them was minuscule. Far more common were the drifters, people barely sentient enough to be alive, who drifted from one chair, one bumper sticker slogan, one fad diet, one store, one table, to the next with little conscious understanding of how they'd arrived.

Even as a little girl, Mary had never been at risk of taking that path. Politicians had been her heroes. How could they not be? Impassioned faces and stirring speeches commanding television cameras and changing the world. She'd longed to be one of those people who had an idea and then brought it into life. In her village, hope had been a poor commodity. Every time she moved, she bumped into a wall someone had built to hold her in. Women in head scarves with arms full of babies, grandmothers with eyes full of lost stories, unfinished houses tacked up with Tyvek, icy water warming on the stove, the smell of frying fish.

As an adolescent, she'd learned that there were as many walls in the cities as in the villages, though their stones looked different. At home, at least, she'd possessed some intrinsic value, she'd been born connected to the earth. In the city, worth was sparingly dispensed based on saleability and looks, connections were the stuff of bank accounts and social networks. Mary quickly realized that she'd never be one of those camera-faces inspiring strangers and writing laws. She was too short, too round, her eyes too narrow, her hair too straight, her tongue too sharp and clever, her pockets too bare.

Likely many women were so discouraged by this reality that they gave up, went home, fell into the common paths that brought at least contentment if not happiness, but Mary was indomitable fireweed to their crushable violets. She doubled down on her studies, confident that ability and will would carry her as far as she wanted to go. She went from speechwriter to campaign manager in record time, sought-after and feared alike. She learned that the politicians she'd imagined so powerful were more like hothouse flowers, requiring constant care and protection to maintain their showy blooms and curated fragrances. Mary was a master gardener, greenhouse and garden both her unquestioned domain.

Actually liking, much less loving, her little seal pup had come as a surprise. It had long been a struggle not to fall into casual contempt for these camera queens who required so much care to survive the hot lights and incessant barrages of criticism, but the seal pup had been different. Her innate loveliness had been a function of her passionate heart and idealistic mind, and somehow Mary had found herself in this willowy, beautiful creature who was handed all the power that Mary had been denied. It would have been easy to envy and hate her, but it was easier to adore her. And sometimes, after a particularly brutal day of questions and defenses from ravens and coyotes, the weariness and doubt in her dark eyes looked just like Mary's own lost Ryska. There'd been no doubt that this was the story Mary had been waiting for all her life, the story that would change the world.

So when the ravens finally ate crow—Mary grinned to herself—and came pecking at her door, she'd been gracious as she'd acquiesced to what they thought was their own plan. They'd been in control of the party for so long, they didn't even notice any inroads on their power structure. From their point of view, she knew, they were propping up a caricature they could use to pander for votes without ever giving up their iron-fisted stranglehold on the state. It would never have occurred to them that a Native woman could take anything from them they weren't willing to give, especially not one defined by loss and grief as she was. They were banking on the public sympathy for her weakness and sadness winning them votes, oblivious to the steel that lurked beneath her placid face and smiling cheeks.

They were desperate, of course. When the seal pup had disappeared after her election win four years ago, a new election had been held in a hurry. Totally unprepared for that scenario, their only viable candidate was the pup's exact opposite: a party old-timer whose decades-old oil connections and good ol' boy persona lost all the cross-over votes that the pup had managed to steal. Alaska didn't suffer liberals well, though, and the loss had been a close one. Mary wouldn't offer the sex appeal that had lured some of the male voters to the seal pup's ticket, but her non-threatening grandmotherly appearance reassured the hardliners that she was malleable enough to provide an acceptable cover face. As far as they were concerned, she was a one-issue wonder, dedicated to the cause to which her own daughter had been lost, easily molded to fit the rest of their ticket. No one would mind a grieving mother thoroughly distracted by the search for her child. As far as the ravens were concerned, it was the perfect ticket.

Mary didn't mind playing along.

What they discounted was her hate.

She'd been a fair-minded woman once. Members of all parties had known they could seek out her when they were looking to discard their bumper stickers and actually get something done. She had a gift for finding compromise and sniffing out common goals, a talent for spin that made both sides look like principled statesmen instead of desperate scrappers. A true believer in the process, she'd delighted in the subtleties of the give-and-take, exulted in those rare moments of perfect synchronicity when the common good was served by what the foolish public thought sworn enemies.

Political sparring served the basest of public hungers in much the same way as football rivalries or boxing matches. The pageantry, the pretended hate, was vital to the fun. The fact that players changed teams all the time and only made more money by doing so was beside the point. Watch the players, watch the players, and never ask where all the ticket fees are going or how they've convinced you that giving strangers millions of dollars for running back and forth across the same field over and over is what makes you happy.

She'd been proud of what they'd managed to accomplish, imagined that the small triumphs were all part of an inexorable progress. But when she needed more than a small triumph—when she needed a big save—players and spectators alike vanished.

Ryska hadn't been polished enough to merit public favor. Pretty but cheap and soiled by their standards, she was no Indian princess singing with deer and promising a direct connection to the Great Spirit. She'd been young and broken, caught up in drugs and an abusive white boyfriend. As far as the ravens and coyotes were concerned, it was too bad that she'd disappeared, but what did she expect? She clearly hadn't valued her own life much; she couldn't expect them to place a higher premium on it than she did. There wasn't even much point in wasting resources on the search when they all knew the outcome. Maybe her boyfriend had killed her, maybe a drug dealer, maybe a jealous woman, the who really didn't matter. Or the how. She was just another embarrassingly flawed Native girl reaping what she sowed. No one wanted to play the race card, but come on—all you had to do was look at the substance abuse statistics, the unemployment numbers, and you could hardly be surprised that these girls dropped like carrion. How long could white people be expected to feel guilty over something that happened decades ago? Nobody was pushing them off their land today. If they weren't making it now, it was because they didn't want to. And so the rhetoric went, whether spoken aloud or merely whispered behind cupped hands.

Mary had thought she was too old and crafty to be disenchanted, but she'd been wrong. She'd thought she'd paid her dues, earned her place, merited some kind of loyalty from the society she'd given her life to, but that had been mere naïveté on her part. When Ryska disappeared, Mary'd been just another other to the ravens and coyotes and cormorants, her anger and grief predictable but unsympathetic. White men got defensive when she pointed out that over ninety percent of sexual violence against Native women came from white men. White women wanted to believe that her problem was not their problem, that some inescapable difference made her daughter vulnerable and kept their own safe. Native people were too exhausted by old angers and old griefs to join her fight. All the connections, all the differences she thought she'd made, abandoned her, shamed by her loss. She was utterly alone, until she found her furious, beautiful, passionate little seal pup.

Magically, the seal pup had managed to accomplish what Mary could not. Her beauty and grace had stirred the protective instincts of men who wanted to believe they were saviors and not exploiters. She'd offered hope to women who'd felt safer giving up than fighting a losing battle. She'd enchanted the coyotes with their cameras and inspired cormorants to prove themselves. And now, she was the cause they could all embrace, the cause that Mary would use to take her own seat in the Senate.

And once there, they'd find that she was much more than the one-cause cardboard cutout they hoped to parade around as proof of their own humanity. Losing Ryska had shown her what they truly were, and Mary did not forget. They would find her a formidable enemy, and she would find her little rabbit. Somehow. Whatever it took.

The election was still two years out, but now was the time to start building a platform and winning back the votes the party lost last time. Mary dressed herself with all the care she'd once lavished on her seal pup. As a campaign manager, she'd maintained fierce control over her appearance as well, with not so much as a nod to her Native heritage. She'd kept her image strictly professional, reliable and unthreatening to politicians and party members who otherwise might have worried that her interests didn't align with their own. Now she costumed herself with quiet reminders of her origin story, wearing her Orthodox cross on the outside of her blouses instead of underneath, shell earrings, a single plait in her hair. She attended breakfasts with village grandmothers, lunches with business owners, dinners with coyotes and ravens. But the two accessories she still carried with her everywhere were the photos of Ryska and her seal pup.

Her one lingering disappointment, for which she supposed she ought to be grateful, was the general disinterest of the cormorants. Her new political schedule made her trips back and forth to the cabin tighter and more difficult to manage, but no one seemed to notice her frequent travels and consistent disappearances. There'd been a cursory questioning back when the pup had first disappeared, of course, but no one ever seriously considered her so much as a person of interest, much less a suspect. Some part of her had expected, with her relaunch into the public spotlight, that a stray cormorant somewhere might take notice of her, but they discounted her as easily as a villain as they had as a grieving mother. Which was fine, really; she needed more time with her pup if she was to uncover the truth about her Ryska, but she couldn't help a vague sense of discontent.

And she was getting closer to her little rabbit. She could feel it. Not long after the pup's disappearance, Mary had gotten a letter from one of Ryska's friends, an older woman who wrote Mary from prison, asking her to visit. The woman, who looked twenty years older than she was, had had little to offer. She'd rambled on about Ryska's boyfriend/dealer and the violent tendencies of which Mary was already aware. By the time she left the concrete walls behind, she still didn't know if the woman had been motivated simply be a desire to feel important on the outside, or if she'd hoped that Mary would use her influence with the parole board to release her early. Mary had no intention of helping the woman, but she was reassured to think that people behind bars were saying her daughter's name and recounting her story. Somewhere, someone knew what had happened. Someone was trying to fight their way out from under their burden of guilt. If Mary could keep Ryska alive in their hearts, if she could remind them, every day, that a mother still waited for her child to come home, then maybe one day someone would do the right thing.

That hadn't been the only lead. She'd waited impatiently for Ryska's ex to come in off the rigs, only to learn that he'd flown Outside. He wasn't much one for social media, but his sister was, and Mary was able to keep tabs on him well enough to know that he was currently in Montana and didn't seem to have any plans to return to Alaska. Mary was careful never to make accusations, but every few weeks she posted a photo of Ryska to his sister's page, with a generic plea for anyone with any information to come forward.

After all, she couldn't have lived with that sort of guilt herself. She didn't imagine that his family could either. If they suspected, if he was the answer to this terrible question, eventually they'd crack. Wouldn't they? How could another woman—a sister, a mother—remain indifferent to the plight of a daughter?

Speaking of daughters, this afternoon was her monthly lunch with the seal pup's parents. She hadn't known them as much more than props before the election, but after the pup disappeared, they'd become allies and friends, suffering the sort of battle wounds that only bereaved parents bear. Like the pup herself, they had a put-together polish that Mary had never had, but all the differences that would have kept them distant before fell away before their shared horror and grief. Not only that, but they were staunch political allies. The Athabascan tribe was not to be sneered at when it chose to mobilize, and for them, the pup was much more than a mere poster child.

Mary fingered her cross as she strode up the stairs to the brewery patio. Early fall, it was already too cold for dining al fresco, but that only guaranteed them privacy in the otherwise teeming pub. The pup's parents were waiting for her when she reached the top of the stairs, three narrow glasses full of amber liquid on the table. The wait staff here knew their routine, and they wouldn't hover too close once they'd placed their orders. Not that this place was known for its stellar service, anyway. Mary supposed that at least one reason they'd settled on this location was its propensity for distractions. The hard truths they all carried demanded so much attention, all the time. A little noise, a little boister, a little pretense at a normal life was good for them all. From the outside, they looked like three friends enjoying a relaxed afternoon out. Inside, they were beached whales, bloated with death, desperate to escape the currents of life but perpetually cast back into their grief by well-meaning rescuers.

Mary ordered a burger, as she always did, just to save herself the tedium of reading the menu and pretending to care what she ate. Since she'd lost her appetite—when had that been? A year ago? Two? Three?—she'd lost weight as well, which only made her that much more presentable to the coyotes. She'd never be slender, wouldn't have recognized herself if she were. She ate for fuel only these days, fuel and appearances.

Appearances. She gazed at the pup's parents' faces, measuring the new lines that had collected since their last lunch together, the new grey hairs, the new despair. She knew exactly what they felt. You could only hope and yearn and pray so much. Long before your mind wanted to let you move on, your body insisted. Eventually there would come a night that you would sleep all the way through again. One day you would realize that you were looking forward to something, something stupid, something petty, and you would hate yourself for that brief joy. But then another brief joy would intrude, and then another. Eventually you would begin to re-order your life, not around what had been, but what would be. First an hour would pass without thinking of the lost one, then three hours. Perhaps an entire afternoon. And then all your grief and fear would be overborne by terrible guilt, the self-loathing that only a survivor knows.

It had taken her longer than them to reach that awful tipping point, where the brain shifted from recovery to survival, but then, Ryska had been all she had. These parents had each other, and she suspected some latent sense of fealty had driven them out from under their grief to care for each other. That was no relief, though, she knew; it only made their burden of guilt that much greater. Not only were they alive and healthy and free, they even had the added comfort of companionship, while their daughter was out there alone.

It had been different for her. She'd had no one to distract her, no one to help her, no one to comfort her. She hated the women who came to her with their own stories of missing daughters, despised them for imagining that she could be consoled by the commonality of tragedy. They had given up. They had accepted the loss. She would not. She would never. She flagellated herself with Ryska's memory, her punishments the more severe for every unwary moment of happiness or forgetfulness. Still, despite her best efforts, her treacherous body learned to take respite, delighting in the long hours at the gym or the walks along the trails. And she hated herself for every minute of peace.

So she could not help but be sympathetic to the suffering of these two. There could be no reprieve from this sort of pain. Their friendship was predicated not on any hope for relief, for succor, but on the sure knowledge that there would be none.

The father was taciturn, the mother gregarious, but all their words were only the same.

Where is she?

When is she coming home?

Who am I without her?

Where am I without her?

Mary parried with words as nonsensical and empty as their own, whose shapes varied but their import was the same.

Where is Ryska?

It was all she said, all she had said for fourteen years, no matter what anyone thought they heard.

The after-lunch embraces were as surreal as always. It was like wrapping her arms around herself. Lax breasts pressed against her own, empty belly crying out for its stolen fruit, the unexpected strength of arms clinging to what was long lost, the scent of woman-hair whose promise of refuge could not be kept. The fierce, bitter handshake and sliding gaze of the father who didn't know who he could possibly be if he wasn't the father who protected his daughter. If he wasn't the man who saved his baby.

Mary had no name to give him. She had no name for herself. The only name that mattered was Ryska, and she recounted that name, over and over, the mantra of her hours.

Time was slipping away from her. It was only three in the afternoon, but this time of year, daylight was scant. She wanted to get out to the cabin before darkness fell in earnest. Moose tended to congregate on the roads at night, and everyone knew someone who'd met an abrupt end courtesy of a moose through the windshield. She preferred to keep night driving to a minimum, although that wasn't a luxury she could always afford in the wintertime. The pup needed tending, and her new responsibilities sometimes meant shifting to later hours than she liked.

She stopped by the house to pick up the supplies she'd packed for her trip that morning. It had taken months of waiting—grandmothers couldn't be rushed—but the artist she'd commissioned for *The Girl Who Married the Moon* had finally finished a new book for her. The pup had worn the first one nearly to shreds. It was a shame. Works of art like these were priceless, unspeakably rare, but Mary didn't have the heart to restrict the pup's access to the one thing that brought her so much joy. The new book, *The Girl Who Searched for Her Lover*, was as beautiful as the first, although its illustrations were far grimmer.

Like *The Girl Who Married the Moon*, this story was familiar to Mary, although the language was as strange as it had ever been to her. She took a bitter satisfaction in knowing that while the Russians might have robbed most of her people of their language long ago, she was empowering this grandmother who had been trapped in the isolation of her tongue for so long. Even if only she and the pup would ever read the woman's words aloud, without comprehension, their voices would lend life and strength to words that would otherwise lie silent and buried on the page.

Mary didn't know how much of the story the pup could gather from the illustrations, but if she understood at all, Mary knew it was the sort of story the pup would love. A tale of devotion and vengeance, of a woman who does not wait on men to save her, but instead avenges the death of her lover and saves herself through courage and cunning. The sort of woman the pup had wanted to be.

As she hoped last year when she'd brought the first book to her pup, the simple magic of language had restored much of the pup's lost luster. It was a gamble, of course. The danger was that the seal pup might revisit her earlier rebellious inclinations, but so far, that possibility had not materialized. The pup still demonstrated the slavish affections that had disturbed Mary when they'd first emerged, but her eyes no longer gazed on Mary with that dull emptiness. She laughed at odd moments, kindled by sparks Mary couldn't see, and had made constant companion of Ryska's little stuffed rabbit. The pup's newfound incarnation resembled madness, but Mary knew the difference between the world within and the pretenses without. Her little pup was no longer merely surviving her rebirth; she was thriving, growing, learning, changing. Much as Mary prized her own safety, the sanctity of her plan to find Ryska, she had no intention of robbing the pup of who she was becoming.

She wasn't a monster, after all.

She carefully laid the book on the passenger seat, wrapped in tissue paper and ribbon so the pup would have the fun of opening it. She filled the back seat with a plastic tote crammed with groceries and toiletries, filled her tumbler with coffee, and set off down the road, eyes peeled for wandering moose in the twilight. She made it to her pull-out without incident, and swiftly transferred her bounty to the back of the ATV that waited for her under a camouflaged tarp, slipping the precious book into the backpack she slung over her shoulders.

An hour later, as she approached the cabin door in the darkness, she could hear the excited huffing and little squeals of the seal pup on the other side of the door. Mary knew the pup would happily barrel out into the drive to meet her if she'd been allowed, but Mary wouldn't risk it. As unlikely as it might be that she'd be followed out here, it was still possible. So the pup was under strict orders to remain inside and wait there. While Mary was away, she permitted the pup to wander outside as long as she stayed within sight of the cabin. Worst case scenario, Mary could always protest plausible deniability, but that would be impossible if someone actually spotted them outside there together.

Nothing tied Mary to the cabin on paper, but she could claim good reason to be there if anyone questioned her. Constructed as a hunting cabin in the '50s, back when homesteaders were showing up in droves and then heading back Outside just as quickly, it had belonged to Ryska's boyfriend's grandfather. He'd proven up on the place, but two years after getting the deed, his wife had refused to spend one more winter in the Frozen North. They'd gone home to Montana but hadn't been able to unload the property on anyone else at the time. Too remote, too inaccessible. Even when Ryska's boyfriend had shown up in the state to chase the oil money, he'd never spent any time there.

Naturally the cabin had been the first place Mary had thought to search when Ryska disappeared, but the place looked as if it'd been deserted for a hundred years when she'd shown up. She hadn't given up, though, coming back weekend after weekend to search the surrounding forest and muskeg. The place had strangely begun to feel like her own. As the seeds of her plan began to germinate, she'd visited even more frequently, at all days and hours, to make sure the cabin was abandoned as it seemed to be. Eventually she'd begun fixing it up—only on the inside, so that any unlikely hunters in the area wouldn't be tempted to take shelter inside.

She gently set the seal pup aside, stroking her hair, taking quiet pleasure in the now-shoulder length mass of dark shining tresses. She'd wondered, at first, if it wouldn't be better to keep her shorn, but she'd finally dismissed the idea as too Hebraic in its mythology. The pup trusted her now, loved her, understood that they were in this together. There was no need for unceasing subjugation.

The pup happily tore through the tote and its treats when Mary slid her treasure out of the backpack and laid it on the table. The pup froze, eyes fixed on Mary with almost painful hope. Mary smiled and nodded. Reverently, hands shaking, the pup carefully untied the ribbon, unwrapped the delicate tissue paper. Tears fell on the stiff canvas cover, magnifying the deliberate black block-print lettering that neither of them could understand.

On tiptoe, as if a sudden movement might cause the book to vanish, the pup crossed the room to the window where her little rabbit stared out on the icy fields with button eyes. Gingerly the pup held the book up in the toy's vision before clasping the stuffed animal to her chest in a paroxysm of delight. Then she fairly leapt back to Mary's side, tugging fiercely on her arm in an effort to drag her over to the bed where the pillows were already propped, story-ready.

Sweet happiness welled up in Mary's chest, overpowering her with its un-expected joy. Swift on its heels came the guilt, the rage, that stole her breath and set her heart staggering. Furious, she wiped at the tears that filled her own eyes, determined not to take her self-loathing out on this innocent. She gestured to the table, to all the food she'd brought, but the pup shook her head vigorously, wav-ing the book in a clear message.

Mary slipped into the covers beside the seal pup, drew her close. The pup's head rested on her ample breasts, all her attention focused on the book in Mary's hand. Mary drew in the scent of the pup's hair and tried not to remember all the nights she had spent reading to Ryska. Tried not to forget.

Mary opened her mouth, drank in the words, spilled them out again in a lyric her ear couldn't hear and her heart couldn't misunderstand.

This girl would save herself. She believed. This girl would save herself.

YEAR FOUR
Noni Begay

Noni dug her hands into the dirt until she felt the earth clutch back at her fingers. She'd grown dangerously fond of her little garden. Dangerous, because she knew it was as impermanent as every other joy Mary allowed her. Noni doubted the Mary-mother knew how sharp her own teeth were, how her claws dug into flesh with every caress, and Noni was wary of new wounds. Even if Mary permitted her to keep tending her little patch, though, autumn would arrive and steal it away, leaving her stranded in a world all grey and brown, black and white.

Till then, Noni spent her days in the flowers. She had other crops, too: a handful of potatoes sleeping under the dirt, beets and carrots, a few heads of cabbage. Rhubarb had come and gone. Along the verge of the forest wild blueberries and raspberries rambled, and later, tiny cranberries would be her last crop, gleaming scarlet among frost-tipped fallen leaves under drowsing trees. She'd learned early on to carefully ration the small supplies Mary left her, but Mary's returns were erratic, impossible to predict. Often she ran out of food entirely a day or two or three before Mary arrived with groceries, and more often still was down to just an apple or a few crackers a day.

When hunger gnawed at her, she tried to stay outside of the paper walls, tried to keep her feet to Beaver Woman's path where appetite was only a phantasm, but sometimes panic rose all the same. What if Mary didn't come back this time? What if she was alone, forever? How would she survive the long dark winter?

People were made of earth, made to be one with the earth, she tried reminding herself. Her people had survived on this land for millennia. Surely she could survive as well. Her hobbled gait was a problem. She couldn't travel far, couldn't venture more than a few feet into the river for fear of being tumbled and drowned. Mary kept the cabin empty of anything Noni could use as a weapon. The nearest thing she had was the one flimsy trowel she'd been given along with seed packets and plant starts. Bringing down a moose or a bear was an impossibility. She could build a trap to catch fish, maybe. But she had no means of salting them. She could keep herself alive in the brief summer. But after that?

Mary even chopped her wood for her, taking the ax back with her on every trip. And she only left Noni the minimal clothing required to survive the cabin, not the survival gear she would need to spend time in the freezing temperatures outside, the heavy wet snow and glassy ice.

Noni shook her head, imagining her fear scattering like drops of water. Mary-mother would be back. And today, the sun shone. Winter was a distant threat. She would find a way through this winter, like she had every one before. Mary would not abandon her to face its privations alone.

Noni pulled her hands free of the earth's grip and wiped her hands on her thighs. Bleeding-hearts, peonies, hostas, asters, roses, and hydrangea meandered around her. She knew Mary thought they were busy work, keeping her occupied with purposeless tasks so she would forget to escape, but she didn't care. Mary was wrong, on both counts.

There was nothing purposeless about coaxing life and color from the patient earth, its belly swollen with seed it ached to bear. A touch, a kiss, a caress, and animus sprang forth, spilling out of her arms, covering every inch of ground. This was power.

Every unfurling bud, every reaching stalk, stoked the fires in Noni's own womb. She burned, a clear, steady flame that ate away more and more of the paper walls. At night when she lay on the narrow bed, the roof curled away into ash, leaving her body bare to the midnight sun that held the falling lights of weeping stars in abeyance till darker nights. The walls of the cabin tumbled into embers, and the stalwart bodies of the spruce formed the fortress of her dreams. Rabbit wandered farther and farther away, often not returning till Noni woke. Beaver Woman dressed Noni's pillow with fish bones and pinecones.

Now, as she sat among the flowers, Noni built an army of the dead under the spreading leaves and tangled thorns. Tiny sticks speared into ground, topped with pinecones or fish vertebrae, formed a macabre advance force, impaled heads of her enemies concealed by nodding blooms.

The Mary-mother brought a new book.

Noni thought her heart would burst when she saw it. New words rolled off the page and took shape in the air, sent their echoes trembling through Noni's veins. Noni devoured the story told in bright paint on thick paper and made it her own, claimed the crudely-drawn figure with long black hair and raven eyes as herself. Eagerly she examined every scene, distilled its story from the images there.

A young girl sent a hunting party to its death at the hands of her lover, a mighty cannibal. After waiting long enough to be certain of their fate, she kayaked down-river to join the cannibal, but she found his affections divided. His hunts were shared with three other women, a dishonor the young girl would not countenance. She slew all three women and left their corpses for him to find. When he returned to the barabara they shared, she taunted him with her magic until he surrendered his weapons to her hand. Her anger was not soon slaked: she tormented her lover with stories, whispering into his ear when he would sleep, forcing him to stay awake through five moons.

When he finally fell into a deep exhausted sleep, the young girl took her knife and beheaded him as he had beheaded the hunting party she sent him. She took his weapons and paddled back upriver to her village, imbued with all his power. She was not a sister or a wife or a grandmother; she was a creature of hunger and ability, a harvester of blood, a seductress and a crone.

So Noni beheaded her enemies, too, and impaled them under the garden flowers. She imagined the hunting party had thought themselves fierce and able. They had thought they served the girl's needs, thought they hunted to keep her and the village fed. But she had despised them for their uselessness, judged them only good enough to fill her lover's belly.

Noni's mind shifted uneasily, names and images moving under the surface of the opaque waters of memory. She, too, had known hunting parties, hadn't she? Men and women decked in armed regalia, who shook hands and shouted speeches and marched down swept streets. Hunters who did not know the woods, archers with dulled arrowheads and broken fletching, trackers with fogged eyes and stuffed ears. Like the young girl in the story, she must have loved them too, for a while. But now she knew them for the fatuous wastes they were, and her contempt found ease only in their expiration. She would gladly deliver them to the cannibal, listen as their bones crunched and tissue squelched between his teeth. They had not found her. No one had found her.

Grimly she stabbed a pinecone too hard, and the little stick split.

Mary-mother thought she was sleeping inside herself. Mary-mother thought she was tamed. But she was only waiting. One day her magic would be strong enough, and she would kill the cannibal, too.

She impaled the pinecone more carefully, set the little spike in the dirt under the arch of fuchsia bleeding-hearts. It was time she wrote her own story.

She began in the woods.

Beside the shallow riverbed, starved now of its bounty beneath the stark summer sun, Noni laid out stories built of sticks on stone. Rabbit could not read, and Beaver Woman eschewed all the trappings of the paper world and its flimsy scaffolds of words. Still Noni tried to reach them, reading the words aloud over the quiet chatter of the river. Rabbit merely watched her, with dark uncomprehending eyes. Beaver Woman retreated to the dam that stretched over the water, looking away across the hills as her feet dangled in the current.

The sound of her own voice frightened her. Noni was sure her vocalizations matched the shapes she'd laid out, but they fell harsh and foreign in her ears. Their hard edges jangled against her thoughts, tumbling out of order. She tried reciting the words she'd memorized from Mary-mother's readings, but the English and *Unangam Tunuu* tangled up in each other's arms till she couldn't tell which was which or what any might mean. Frantically she ran her hands up and down her limbs, tore off her clothes and examined her bare flesh. Had she become beast? Was there nothing left of woman, after all?

But her arms and legs still looked human, her face felt smooth, her teeth unserrated. Slowly she replaced her clothes, wondering if they, too, were only lies she told herself, remnants of a name she no longer wore. Maybe they were. Maybe there was little left of a person about her, and yet her flesh was too weak and pathetic to survive without them. Her identity was fading, dissolving into muskeg mud and the foggy light of the midnight dawn, and still she had no place in any pack. Rabbit and Beaver Woman suffered her company, but they were not her tribe. They were made of stories they never told, ate meat she could not share.

She wanted to stay in that place and watch all her words slip away in the river as she threw them in, one stick at a time, but the mosquitoes chased her away when she had only half-way demolished her little book on the bank. That night as she lay in bed, she pictured them still lying there, crying out their gibberish to the slumbering sky.

The next morning, she returned to her garden and tried to pretend the voices of her flowers were all she heard. For a while, she'd taken comfort in the not-quite-comprehensible music drifting from their petals. Now, it frustrated her, taunting her as her mind scrabbled at the edges of meaning, never quite catching hold. Gasping for air, heart rattling frantically in her chest, she pushed herself up, clapping her hands over her ears and running for the cabin.

She was being unwound from herself, she was losing her name, losing her mind, losing her senses. Or rather, losing her sensibility, with senses alone left for navigation. Noni wrapped her arms around her knees and rocked back and forth, clinging to the hard bite of the wooden floor into her hip bones as proof she was still here, still singular, still distinct.

She'd never been so glad to hear the roar of Mary-mother's engine as the ATV approached. Had she known somehow? Had she felt that Noni was slipping away from herself? Noni sprang to her feet, fairly dancing in her anticipation till Mary came through the door and she threw herself into her arms.

Mary dropped her bags without hesitation and gathered Noni to her broad chest, stroking her hair and rocking her gently side to side as she hummed a tuneless melody against Noni's head. Warmth and safety spread through Noni's body and her knees weakened, overwhelmed with the sudden reassurance that she was a person, a person who was known and recognized and beloved. Even if it was only the cannibal who knew her. Only the cannibal who loved her.

Something rebellious stirred in Noni at that thought. Hadn't there been other people who loved her? Might there be other people still?

No. How could that be true? How could anyone love her and leave her here, to this terrible silence? Only one person pursued. Only one person stayed. Only one person came.

Noni loved Mary-mother at least as much as she hated her. One day, when the knife finally plunged to its home, she would weep more than anyone.

But she would still wield the knife.

She just needed to remember her name, remember her story.

Mary-mother put her away at last. Noni hovered nearby, drawing as sustenance Mary's assumption of her reality. Mary touched her hair, Mary cooked her fried fish, Mary tucked her in the bed and piled blankets high around her. Most important of all, Mary climbed in beside her and read to her from The Books.

As the harsh sunshine subsided to a violet twilight, Noni traced Beaver Woman's watching eyes in the log beside her bed. She needed Beaver Woman to survive. She could not walk this land alone. But she could not let Beaver Woman take her words. Beaver Woman wanted Noni to become fox, become hare, become salmon and slip away, indistinguishable from all fauna.

As lonely as she was, Noni needed to be lonelier. She had to make Beaver Woman understand she would always be stranger and sojourner. Immeasurably grateful for permission granted to travel through worlds not her own, she must find a way home all the same. It would be so easy to allow her blood to become water, become river, to make compost of memories and give her strength to the trees. But Noni wanted to keep her blood.

Mary-mother's engine had scarcely fallen into silence as she left, two days later, before Noni had retrieved every can and box of food from the shelves. Gingerly, with shaking hands, she unwrapped the labels from the cans. Any box whose contents were held in a plastic bag was carefully unfolded, its bent edges laid flat. Here, she had paper.

She used rocks to hold down the edges so they would flatten out. A bowl with ground charcoal from the woodstove and water from the muskeg made a basin of ink. She tried using a stick for a stylus but quickly found her finger made a better pen.

It took a couple of days to fill her makeshift notebook. Her words were few, but it was such a trial catching them and pinning down to the pages. Every letter, every sound, seemed a honeybee that flitted away every time she approached, sipping bloom to bloom and forever changing its flavor on her tongue. Her head ached and her eyes felt as if they would never close, their lids stretching farther and farther apart in the effort to see what kept slipping away. Finally her story was complete.

The next step required even more concentration. She could only fit a letter or two on each scrap, and it was paramount she not lose track as she pasted them up on the cabin walls with her toothpaste glue. If she forgot her order, picked up the wrong page, she might never decipher her own meaning again. She created a simple dance, practiced its steps again and again till the choreography required no attention. Finally she was ready to begin hanging her message.

It was a kind of magic, she concluded. Once the words were firmly anchored on the curling labels and cardboard, they held no place in her mind. Following the invisible threads that drew them to their assigned dockets on the wall required the strongest, fiercest spells she could summon. Beaver Woman and Rabbit watched her somberly, their expressionless faces giving neither aid nor discouragement. Only Noni could do this.

By the time she finished her incantation of feet and hands and words and will, she shook so hard she could barely stand. Had she forgotten to eat? Probably. She glanced around her cramped living quarters. Aluminum cans glinted at her from every surface. Yes. Not a one was open. When had Mary left? Two days ago? Three? Four?

Even now, hunger did not rouse. Noni climbed onto her bed, shoulders sinking against the wall beside Beaver Woman's avatar as she gazed on her creation. Satisfaction and power spread in equal measure through her body, filling her belly and soul better than any food. The import of the words she had so painstakingly scrawled out, the import she had lost as soon as the letters took form on paper, now blazed across her mind like wildfire, a smoldering inferno she would not forget again.

I am Noni Begay, and I see the Star-People.

Let the sun shine all the night long. Maybe the Star-People couldn't see her anymore. She did not need them to see her after all; they derived their reality from her, not the other way around. She was the paper and the conflagration, the spirit and the husk, the lost and the found. She would walk both worlds till she reached the bridge that bound them and make her escape.

I am Noni Begay, and I see the Star-People.

YEAR FIVE
Mary Nelson

Something was wrong with the seal pup.

Mary began to question her decision to bring in the books.

At first, it seemed to be working brilliantly. The seal pup, who had grown so dull-eyed and languid, perked right up. She'd been genuinely happy, Mary was sure. Mary had even brought seedlings and a hand trowel to the cabin, and the pup had shown all the signs of becoming a master gardener. The fresh vegetables were good to have, but they served as more of a distraction for the pup than a food source. After all, Mary didn't want the pup to forget on whom she truly relied for her survival. To that end, she'd brought more flowers than food plants, and the pup had elaborately schemed out a beautiful landscape of ebullient color that bloomed in carefully ordered turns, so that the little cabin was always awash in new hues. At first, Mary had worried that the clear evidence of a caretaker might bring some random vagabond to the cabin door, but she needn't have. She was finally relaxing on that score. Five years gone by now, and not a soul had ventured this way. And why would they? No roads, no reason to be out here. No one would ever find them here.

That second book, though. Maybe that was when it had started to go wrong. Oh, the pup had been beside herself with glee when Mary had first read it to her. And at first everything seemed the same. But then the rebellion began.

Mary came home to the cabin to find the walls plastered with food wrappers. The pup had carefully unwound them from canned goods and juice bottles, unfolded cracker and cereal boxes, dusted off and opened out flour and sugar bags. Mary was conscientious not to leave any pens or pencils behind, but the inventive little pup had crafted her own, using charcoal from the wood stove and flower petals and berries from the woods. Then she'd used toothpaste like glue and pasted up page after page of words on the wooden cabin walls, covering every surface that she could.

I am Noni Begay, and I see the Star-People. I am Noni Begay, and I see the Star-People. I am Noni Begay, and I see the Star-People.

Mary saw it for what it was at a glance, of course: open revolt. She kept her usual placid expression grimly plastered to her face as she slowly, methodically, tore down every page and threw them into the fire. The pup wept and pleaded, making an awful racket and hanging on Mary's arms, but Mary shook her off like a louse. It took a while, and she had to do some clambering to reach some of the pages—the pup was several inches taller than Mary—but she destroyed every page. Then she went about the day's business as if nothing had happened.

But her next visit had yielded the same thing. After that, Mary took to removing the wrappers from everything she could. The pup would have to guess at the contents of the cans. When Mary returned to find the walls themselves covered with writing, she snatched up the pup's copy of *The Girl Who Married the Moon* and carried it out to her ATV to put it in the saddlebags. What she'd wanted to do was tear it apart, page by page, and burn it in front of the pup, but even as ragged and dog-eared as it was, Mary couldn't bring herself to destroy the book. Hand-painted, hand-printed, in a language spoken by maybe—*maybe*—three hundred people in the entire world, it was more than a work of art. It was an artifact, a relic, a sacred being with a life of its own. So she merely took it away, tucked it safely in her nightstand drawer with the lock of long, lustrous black hair.

She was stunned, then, to find the walls covered again with words when she returned. She knew the pup had been devastated by the loss of her book—she'd thrown herself on the ground, wailing and tearing at her hair and clothes like a mad thing. Why, Mary fumed, why would she do this again? Didn't she know how much it hurt Mary to punish her like this? All she wanted was for her to be good. To be happy. To be well. Mary's stomach had rolled, sick and sour, as she'd taken the pup's last book out to her vehicle, but she'd had no choice. The pup had to learn.

And now, far from being good or happy or well, the pup was sick. Sick at heart.

Mary blamed herself. She knew that parents had to always be on guard against taking the easy way out. She didn't suppose there was any better feeling than the joy in a child's face when they looked up at you, the warmth that sank all the way into your bones when they wrapped their arms around you and held on tight. She'd craved that with the seal pup, too, and she'd gotten it with the books. But they'd done so much more damage than good in the long run. She wasn't angry with the pup, just exasperated. She was angry with herself for allowing this to happen.

She'd been the bad guy for so long with Ryska at the end. Always scolding, always warning. Sending text after text, call after call, driving round at odd hours to see who Ryska was with, what she was doing. More than once, she'd had to haul her baby out of a "party"—more like a ghastly paper-doll convention, with all the poor papers worn to tissues and shredded with needles, while open windows and cranked heaters blew and jerked them room to room, and blaring music pretended at frivolity but only provoked death to slow-dancing—and race her to an emergency room. Ryska'd always rolled her eyes and sighed when she saw her mother coming, but back in the corners of the dark empty rooms that had become Ryska's gaze, Mary saw relief, maybe even a little hope. She hadn't been able to give up on Ryska then. She wouldn't give up on the pup now. If she had to be the bad guy again, so be it.

But had she gone too far? What was the way out?

The pup didn't greet her when she showed up this afternoon. Panic swelled up in Mary's throat like anaphylactic shock, cutting off her air, in the scant second it took her to unlock the door and enter the cabin. Before, she'd always heard the pup's eager sighs on the other side of the door, her little scrabbling hands so ready to draw Mary into a quick embrace as soon as she made it inside. This time, perfect silence hung in the small clearing, punctuated by birdsong and murmuring trees and nothing else. A few persistent flowers still bloomed, heads bobbing gently in the breeze, but Mary couldn't stop herself from slamming the door open as the lock rattled free.

The pup lay there on the cabin floor, ear pressed to the hardwood, arms and legs splayed like a star. She didn't move when Mary entered. Her eyes were closed, but as Mary dropped to her knees beside her, she could feel the pup's breath rising and falling through the thin fabric covering her back. The pup's one upturned eye opened slowly, gazing on Mary without surprise or interest.

The pup didn't protest as Mary rolled her over, checking her limbs carefully for injury, her skin for heat or clamminess. The pup pulled herself to a sitting position, wrapping her arms around her drawn-up knees and simply looking at Mary. Nonplussed but trying not to betray her anxiety, Mary pushed herself back up to her feet and began unpacking the goods she brought as though nothing were wrong. The pup rose to her feet and drifted across the room to the window where her stuffed rabbit sat, ears drooping, and joined its outward gaze.

Mary was reminded of an article she read long ago in some ragged old Witches' Almanac she had picked up from god-knows-where, that described how a witch would develop a relationship with her familiar. Something she'd found in a second-hand shop and been simultaneously too intrigued and too repulsed not to read it cover to cover. It had seemed so genuine, so frightening, that she'd promptly discarded it after reading and had had trouble meeting the priest's eyes for weeks after. Still, that one article had stuck with her somehow. Maybe because it felt truer than everything else she'd read. Like it harkened back to something she already knew, less alchemy and more wisdom.

The ratty old periodical told of long, quiet hours spent silent and still in the company of the chosen familiar—this one apparently a stuffed rabbit—of gazing into the darkness until the witch no longer saw through her own eyes, but through the familiar's. It was a sort of communion, a kind of listening with the eyes, that sounded not unlike the relationship of Mary's own people with the animals who controlled their livelihood. She too had been taught to listen, to look, to understand, to revere even the lives they took. Especially the lives they took.

Watching her little seal pup stare out the window, her head cocked just like her stuffed rabbit's, Mary imagined for a moment that the pup had become the rabbit, that some sea-change she could only barely glimpse through the surging waves was transforming her pet into something she could no longer tame or understand.

Mary shook her head, brushed her hands vigorously down the thick cotton of her leggings. That was nonsense. Sulking, that's what the pup was doing. Sulking. She'd get over it soon enough. Mary's best bet was to ignore it, like she'd ignored Ryska's tantrums and morose fits when she was a child.

The seal pup grabbed her rabbit and wandered outside into the back meadow where the vegetable garden slumbered for winter. Mary put away the groceries and toiletries—sans wrappers—and cooked a simple supper of shrimp and clam alfredo with garlic toast and a frozen cheesecake that had miraculously survived the bumpy trip in. When she stepped outside to call the seal pup to eat, the creature lay on the cold hard ground in the same position she'd been in when Mary had arrived. It was already dark, of course, so she was little more than a shadow huddled on the earth.

It creeped Mary out. She had the eeriest sensation that the pup was listening, listening to something in the earth that Mary couldn't hear.

Resignedly, Mary crossed the brown grass and weeping fireweed to take the pup by the arm. Like before, the seal pup simply rolled over without protest and rose to her feet, meekly following Mary back into the house. She ate every bite of her meal, but more methodically than with delight. When finished, she cleaned up the dishes then subsided back into her new position on the cabin floor.

Hmph. Two could play at this game, Mary decided, and however patient the seal pup imagined herself, Mary was more patient still. She hadn't acquired the success she had amidst all the sexism and racism that dominated her current political party by being rash or emotional in her responses to conflict. She settled into her rocking chair beside the wood stove and picked up her knitting basket, comforted by the steady, regular clacking of the needles and soft heft of the wool. She told herself that the seal pup was comforted, too, that despite her outward stubbornness, inwardly she was soothed by the company, by the quiet rhythm of creation.

An hour later, she wasn't so sure. The pup still hadn't moved, hadn't acknowledged her existence at all since taking up her position. Irritation welled behind Mary's eyes, sharp and acrid. What was she doing? What point did she think she was proving? Surely she didn't actually hear anything down there. Did she?

Fancifully Mary pictured a long-ago scout, ear pressed to the ground, harkening to some oncoming intruders. Hooves striking the earth, perhaps, or the rumble of a distant train roaring over unseen tracks. Some nonsense out of an old Western movie. Or who knew? Maybe that was a real phenomenon, somewhere. Not here. Muskeg and rainforest didn't carry sound, they swallowed it, sucked it down into wet morass and drowned it there.

Still.... Mary eyed the pup irascibly. The creature looked intent, somehow. Attendant on something Mary couldn't sense.

Unconsciously Mary shifted closer to the lantern light. Darkness pressed in on the tiny cabin from all directions. The long winter had only just begun, but already night far outpaced the day. Once Mary had taken the cycle of the seasons in stride, finding equal beauty in twilight winter days as in the midnight summer suns. Summer brought incredible bounty and abundance, but winter had a unique glory all its own, and she'd reveled in them equally. But glorying in extremes is a luxury that the mother of a missing girl can't afford. Winter and darkness bring constant, nagging, fears that know no retreat.

Is she cold? She must be cold. Is she alone? Is she in the dark? She's afraid of the dark. Does she have socks? Does she have gloves? Where is she sleeping? The snow won't stop falling. Is she already under the snow?

Small questions, maybe, compared to the big mysteries surrounding Ryska's disappearance, but the only questions that seemed to matter when the nights grew long. Now, with the pup prone at her feet, and the firelight scant protection against the cold and the dark, Mary found herself wondering if the pup was listening to Ryska. If somehow, the two lost ones were talking to each other. After all, wasn't that why she'd brought the seal pup here in the first place? To find her lost little rabbit? She'd imagined that would happen through further investigations, more media exposure, more political pressure on what had been an invisible issue, but maybe she'd been wrong. Maybe the pup herself would find Ryska.

Mary shook her head firmly and set her knitting aside. This was utter foolery. She'd been reading too many of the old stories. Her head was doddered with stories of ravens and wolves and moon people and monsters. Although was that really so much crazier than praying to dead saints and asking mothers long dead to protect her child when those mothers had failed to protect their own?

Hastily she crossed herself, kissing the heavy gold cross at her neck in fervent apology. She didn't mean that. And her lack of prayers wasn't due to a lack of faith. Not exactly. She still lit the candles. She still implored the priest for aid. She had simply run out of words for God. He knew. He knew. He already knew. He knew what she had lost, what she wanted, and he knew where Ryska was. If he had intended to help, surely he would have done it years ago. So she would help herself.

God the Father would understand what she was doing, she knew. After all, he had sacrificed his own beloved son to save the world. And she was sacrificing her own beloved seal pup to save Ryska and all the other lost girls out there on whom everyone else had already given up. Once the work of salvation was done, the Son had risen to even greater glory, and so the seal pup would too. Mary just needed to find Ryska first.

The pup opened that one eye, rolled it round to gaze on Mary when she put her knitting aside. Clear and self-possessed, that eye unnerved Mary. She huffed, annoyed with herself, and rose to look out the black window beside the stuffed rabbit.

Nothing to be seen, of course. The firelight cast Mary's own reflection, tired and saggy, back at her. The utter void beyond that window oppressed her until she felt she could scarcely fill her lungs. What might lay out there? No matter how long people had settled in this country, they had never been welcome. Never made the land their own. There were good reasons why the Aleuts clung to the coasts. Some countries were harsh, unforgiving, but Alaska was openly hostile to all comers. That forest floor out there was nothing more than a carpet of death. Tourists raved about the lush tapestry of undergrowth, the wealth of color and life, but Mary saw it for what it was: pure, unadulterated greed. That undergrowth fed on decay, turning over every loss to its own purposes. Even now, Mary clung to her spot in this wasteland. If she left this cabin for a year, for two years, it would be swallowed up, eaten whole by the countryside. Her chest squeezed as the hungry malevolence outside pressed nearer and nearer.

Was Ryska out there, being devoured? Was she already long fallen, her bones tuned to rot, her skin a moss carpet, her eyes mushroom stalks?

Horrified by her own musings, Mary spun from the window only to shriek as she came face to face with the seal pup. Lost in her dark thoughts, she hadn't heard the pup rise from the floor and drift to her side. The pup hardly reacted to Mary's outburst, only patted her arm and drew her to the bed. Her dark eyes, that had been so blank, were warm with sympathy.

Mary didn't understand the pup's change of heart, but she was overwhelmingly relieved that she was off the floor, at least. It had felt as if even the pup were leaving her somehow, retreating into a world Mary couldn't see, listening to voices Mary couldn't hear. In the lumpy bed, under the piles of blankets, with the pup's long arms and legs wrapped around her, Mary was able to sleep without dreaming, the only sounds she heard those of the howling winds and the snoring pup.

The pup's strange listening behavior continued, though. And listening it definitely was. Over the next two days they spent together, Mary would find her wrapped around trees too, ear pressed close to the trunk. Worn out by her mind's twisted meandering of the night before, Mary was weary of pondering now. It didn't matter, in the end, what the pup was doing. What message she thought she was sending. Their course was set. They had a purpose, and they would not be moved.

And it was working. It was.

In the first year of early campaigning, most of the work was accomplished behind the scenes. Mary moved cautiously, on the same track she'd designed so successfully for the pup, five years past. It was vital that the ravens consider her a known quantity, exactly what they'd had in the pup. She lacked the sex appeal that they'd used to draw in some of their male demographic, but she elicited a unique sympathy as a result of her double loss that made up for that weakness. Plus, some people felt downright virtuous voting for the ugly fat woman, as if that proved how un-shallow they were. And Mary had been in the trenches a long, long time. Older, more experienced people who had found the pup too naïve, too polished, too pretty to be trusted, considered Mary the real deal.

She wasn't deceived, though. She understood the real reason the ravens wanted her as the face of their party was that they assumed she would be entirely consumed by her one issue and easily manipulated on all others. That didn't trouble her in the least. They'd find out otherwise when she made it to Washington. One issue? So many, many issues had spiderwebbed to create this powerful, sticky trap that ensnared so many women, and she fully intended to tackle them all. In the meantime, she was better off being underestimated. She'd been underestimated all her life. It was the blessing of the plain girl. Not something the seal pup could ever understand.

Admittedly, playing party favorite took more time than she wanted, but it was well worth the cost. Maybe she was a one-trick pony, after all. At every interview, no matter how small, with tiny village newsletters or online bloggers or national television broadcasters, she still carried those same two photographs with her everywhere and insisted on showing them. Insisted on saying their names. Her plea was always the same. Someone knows something. No one should carry a secret that heavy. However petty the information might seem, however inconsequential, every lead had to be followed. She urged everyone listening or watching to call the authorities with whatever they knew.

And people had called. Mary knew, because the bedeviled cormorants had not-so-subtly complained to her about the influx of crank calls and false leads they got after each of her appearances. As far as Mary was concerned, that meant this was working. She told herself it was like Edgar Allan Poe's "Tell-Tale Heart." Every ominous pound of that heart brought the creature that much closer to his doom. She was that heartbeat. And she would pound, and pound, and pound, until the truth was out.

Little changes, brought about by mothers and grandmothers who had been fighting much longer than she, had already been won. Better communication between agencies, better tracking, more jurisdictional control for native reservations and villages. But Mary couldn't bring herself to celebrate these small wins or name them victories. Perhaps the bodies would be easier to find now, but she wanted the girls saved, not avenged.

Something fetid and sick rotted at the core of society, and she wanted it excised. She wanted all the monsters who fed at its spring ended. She was no young woman, hoping for love, dreaming of quiet cabins and wedding ring quilts. She was an old mother, who had looked on grief with unblinking eyes, and she could swing the scythe without regret. All she wanted was one chance, and she would land her blow.

For now, though, she lent her weight and presence to all the popular movements, supported all the camera-ready causes. They, like her, had mothers with posters of their daughters' faces. They shouted the names of the missing in front of capitol buildings and sang their farewells in drum circles. Secretly, she hated them for their familiar grief. She hated them because, just like her, they had been too weak to protect their children. They had lost. They were now defined only by the absence of what they loved. Just like her.

She hated the knowledge in their eyes when they looked at her, how they knew exactly what she had suffered. She did not flatter herself that her sorrow was singular. Was there anything more common to humanity than death? She knew when they looked at her, they saw sweat-soaked sheets, empty vodka bottles, dirty dishes, unwashed hair, a raw throat and burning eyes. They weren't deceived by her pantsuits and subtle makeup. They looked at her and saw themselves: empty womb, empty arms, empty heart, nothing but a Skinwalker. She looked at them and saw the same, and she hated them as much as she hated herself.

She wasn't ungrateful for all they'd accomplished, but she did equally loathe all the proud photo ops where "activist politicians," "concerned politicians," "sympathetic politicians," posed with regalia-decked Native women as if their grand *noblesse oblige* had once again come to rescue of the poor little savages. As if the core of the problem wasn't the endemic racism their society had created and perpetuated and now used to excuse the travesty of justice that left these women so vulnerable to attack, so bereft of retribution.

She needed to be patient, though, she knew. Look both pitiful and thankful until she won her seat. Surely, by then, Ryska would be home. She'd need time to heal, time to recover and rediscover herself, but eventually, Ryska could take her place at her mother's side and rally the nation to a hard reset on how they looked at Native peoples. How they looked at reservations and villages and the real root causes of the rampant alcoholism, drug use, domestic abuse, and sexual assaults. Today most Americans brushed it aside as them lazy Injuns with their firewater and their entitlement and their excuses. After all, the massacres and the forced marches were over a hundred years gone now, and the Indians had their land and their casinos. What more could they possibly want?

Ryska could help change all that. The seal pup, too. Together, the three of them could lead a concerted attack on all the misconceptions surrounding modern Native life, both in the cities and on Native land. They could form real alliances with Native men, alliances that could transcend any political differences. That, Mary grudgingly conceded to herself, had been one of the seal pup's rallying cries. Mary had taken a grittier view at the time, her personal experiences with men of any skin color leaving her reluctant to seek their aid as anything but pretext, but the pup had won her over. The seal pup had been convinced this was not an issue that women could solve on their own. After all, men had not created the problem alone. They'd been taught and trained and reinforced by the values of their own mothers and wives and sisters as well. The heart of the whole nation had to change, not just the heart of its women, not just the heart of its men, the seal pup had insisted. Only by working hand in hand could real, society-sweeping, change be affected.

Not only had the pup been right, but her point had been saliently proven by her own obnoxious lover. Mary had been the one to insist the pup keep him well out of view till after the election—after all, it was that much harder to win the sex vote if you were taken, and that half-wild fisherman she'd taken up with had hardly fed the fully-leashed pet Indian image that Noni needed for her party leadership. After the pup disappeared, though, he'd burst onto the scene in full living Technicolor. A complete contrast to Ryska's boyfriend, who could hardly be bothered to answer police questioning. Izak had moved on with his life, of course. It had been five years, after all. But he hadn't stopped hounding Mary. It was as if he knew, somehow, that she was far closer to the pup than any law enforcement detective would be. At least once a week, he called. Sometimes with leads or gossip of his own, sometimes just to see if she'd heard anything. Mary didn't imagine that his new girlfriend was too happy about his obsession, but thankfully, that was none of her business.

Still, if she hadn't known it would do more harm than good, she'd have liked to tell the pup that she was right. If the men in these missing girls' lives were half as committed as he was, they might not be missing at all, and certainly more of them would be found.

But that was not a story she could tell the pup. The little seal pup had been terribly fond of her lover, if somewhat cavalier with his heart. Learning she was still anchored in his spirit would make her time here in these storm-tossed waters so much harder. Hope, Mary knew to her sorrow, was the cruelest wound there was. She would never inflict that on her pup.

YEAR FIVE
Noni Begay

Mary-mother—Mary-monster—had stolen all her words again.

Noni had fought so hard to win them back, after the long years of silence. When Mary brought the first Book, Noni clung to every syllable, stored every sound deep in her belly where she digested them again and again. The second Book did more than remind her of who she was: it promised a way out. Noni was no longer a listener, a waiter, a receiver. She was a devourer of cannibals, a shepherdess of Star-People, a navigator of upside-down rivers.

She began writing a new end, but Mary-mother kept erasing it. When all Noni's paper was gone, she wrote on the walls, fixing her identity, her purpose on wood. She would speak herself to life, to power. People told stories because they were true. Stories were true because people told them. Even God called Himself The Word, and not just any word—the word that creates, that breathes and sustains life and keeps the worn edges of the universe knitted together. Mary-mother, with her gold cross and dirty feet, knew that too. How could she deny the divine in Noni, how could she steal away the words that would sustain and knit her together?

But she did.

Noni clung to Mary's thick arm, wrapped herself around her legs, pleaded and begged her not to take The Books away, but Mary did not hear. The Books stayed out in the ATV. The eventide that ought to have been filled with the melody of the *Unangum Tunuu* lay heavy and silent on Noni's chest till the very air felt syrupy and sluggish in her lungs. Mary-mother, Mary-monster, regarded her with patient unconcern as she fought to breathe.

Noni had so narrowly won back her name. Would she lose it now?

Help came unexpectedly. Beaver Woman stood by, silent as always, skeptical and resistant to Noni's yearning for the paper world and its flimsy walls. She held her place in the wood beside Noni's bed as Mary-mother wrapped her in her arms and rocked her to sleep with only the wind and the thrush and the warbler to tell her stories. She regarded Noni's abjection without judgment, bore witness to her bereavement and did not mock her for spending so much of her heart on a purchase certain to decay. She only stood and watched and waited.

Mary drove away. Noni dragged herself outside, to sit in the dust and leaf litter of autumn's casual disregard. The season was a vagabond who cared little for the niceties of the other months. Autumn danced till her shoes were soleless, her dresses ragged, her cheeks red, her chest heaving. She would wear herself out with beauty and never regret the death that chased more swiftly on her heels the faster she ran. Something stirred in Noni as the sweet, dark-tea fragrance of the fallen leaves settled in her veins. What seemed like defeat might be the sweetest rebellion yet. They were not dead, these pages of music fallen from the tree limbs. Only see with what bright tongues they sang their fading couplets: scarlet and gold, russet and sienna.

Beaver Woman came to her then. She drew Noni away, back to the riverbank where crimson salmon still pushed their way up the current. Gently she lay Noni down on her belly on the muddy verge, one ear in the wet silt, one ear open to the sky.

Noni listened.

River did not wait.

River was a troubadour, a wandering shaman long since cast out from his tribe. River was brother but no safe friend.

Water rushed through Noni's bloodstream, a torrent of awakening only scarcely bounded by banks and shores. These stony edges marked nothing more than the emergence of flood, the swelling bounty of mud and stone and sticks churned into a remaking of boundaries, a redefining of limits. Glaciers, whose memory stretched millennia of somnolent observance, offered up their secrets as free gifts, the sweet breath of ancient springs granted without measure to these adolescent currents bold with fury. Mountains sent missives rushing to the sea, love letters bound with shredded mark and curling moss. Stalwart earth gave up its gold and tumbling quartz, while the birches abandoned on the river's banks tossed leaves into its flow like favors tossed to doomed knights bound for combat.

Noni listened to them all. While Beaver Woman sat patiently on her dam, her face raised unquestioningly to the dimming sun, Noni listened. And she remembered.

She remembered the salmon and the trout whispering and chucking about her calves as she played in the cold water, a child humored by her parents, guarded from bears. She had been a child, beloved, so now she must be a woman. She might yet become a salmon or a beaver herself, she supposed, or a flowering alder, but even in becoming she must first be. Even the snowy quartz winking at her from the shallow riverbed knew its own name. It had a birthplace. It traveled a journey, and though it often altered, it would not unbecome. She was at least as real as the quartz. Without raising her head from the muddy water, she reached down, grasped the bony knob of her own knee.

See: she too had her prisms, her edges.

When she fell in and out of sleep, Beaver Woman lifted her out of the river's arms, walked her back to the cabin and its poor comforts. Winter followed quickly on autumn's heels, a season of no more notoriety in Alaska than spring. Both were merely the hem of the garment, but oh, how bright and deft their brief needlework.

Even in the grim and bleak nights of snow and ice and rain—all winter was night, regardless of the poor incursions of soft, apologetic light into a few of the middling hours—Beaver Woman taught Noni the languages of the spirit worlds. Spirit only because they were more than dirt, but they were all dirt, too— the worlds of trees and rocks and muskeg and snow. Perhaps there was no paper world after all. Perhaps all worlds were paper and all worlds were spirit. Maybe Noni had misunderstood Beaver Woman's contempt for the words she practiced. Maybe Beaver Woman only waited for her to learn more languages.

Trees were like children. Noni wrapped herself tightly around the spruce and the birch and the cottonwood, bent her ear to the whispered giggles of the wild raspberry and devil's club. So much newer than the rivers or the rocks, they regaled her with misadventures and stunted sallies. The oldest among them was merely adolescent by any other standard. Even so, their stories were so much older than any Noni knew. She clung laughing to their limbs, spellbound by the incantations they muttered to bring forth new leaves or retreat into a slumberous trance, wrapped in ice and dreaming of sun. They told her how to carry strength and life, cell by cell, down dark tunnels and force them into the bellies of reluctant sleepers.

Ice retreats before the sun and advances again without warning. What today bursts boldly into life tonight lies dark and limp, all vigor stolen by the cold. But the grief of darkness lends no remorse to the bold delight of day. So the leaf withers, so the bud dies, frozen in all its aborted brilliance. Still it did live. Still its fragrance lingers on the hour. The trees do not count years by the number of leaves they hold tight to their limbs. They measure time only in rings, in the advance and retreat of the tides.

Noni did not need time to keep her green. She only needed to allow it and regard its browning without fear. She clung to the trees until the bark left tattoos on her cheeks. Her feet followed the meandering of the roots. She felt the warmth of the earth's ovens rising through the ice, through her curling toes. More magic waited here than she could see, but if she listened long enough, she could hear its notes climbing and falling on the staff.

Noni even listened to the cabin, though its tales were darker, grimmer, than she wanted to hear. She laid her ear against the worn, scuffed floorboards and felt the memories of the wood reverberating through her outstretched limbs, her lax belly. Everything sweet here tasted sour on her tongue, the rancid indulgence of something fetid in the sugar. She closed her eyes against the powdery pastels of the wintry light and inhaled the rotten secrets rising from the floor.

Here love was a dead porcupine moldering under the leaves, a rabid shrew scuttling against the corners with claws and teeth. The belly of a moose calf ripped open by a bear's claw, a heap of blueberries left to bloom white and black with mold. Husks of spiders frozen in the frost, dangling from their broken webs, a paper wasps' nest, fallen and shattered.

Noni smelled the dank sweat of sex and fear and meth mingled with longing and contempt, a perfume of roses and feet and blood. Rabbit stayed close as Noni listened, mesmerized by the quiet monotone rambling on and on under the voices of the wood and earth and sky.

She knew this voice, she realized. Recognized the broken timbres, even though she had never heard it in life.

Poor Mary had been right, after all. She was not so far from her daughter as she had come to fear.

Noni sat up, met the gaze of Rabbit who had waited so long to be heard.

It was not as simple as that, of course. Even rabbits who have been women are not easily understood by women who think to tame rabbits. But now Noni knew what she was listening for.

She was an earnest novitiate. Even when Mary came and tried to coax her back into her docile state, Noni practiced her meager devotions. She did her best to humor Mary-mother, to allow her some small incursions, but she needed to listen. She needed to hear. Mary-mother could only move in deceits because she had swallowed deceits. Noni followed after truths.

It was hard to allow old terrors, old agonies, to stretch their limbs inside her own. Hard to listen to a voice more frightened, more lonely, than her own. Hard to follow the trail of breaths to their end. Hard to paint inside her own skin what she had thought to billboard, to bumper sticker, to proclaim her way to triumphant ticker tape.

When spring came, Noni followed Rabbit to a fallen tree trunk deep in the forest, overgrown with moss and ferns and bursting with mushrooms. Beaver Woman accompanied them a short while, but she lingered when they reached a granite outcropping. Beaver Woman climbed the rock and sat with her back to them as they pushed on, her eyes fixed on the shifting swaths of blue sky revealed by the swaying branches. Part of Noni wanted to stay with her, to look on cerulean heavens and turn her back on what waited beneath the dark necrotic earth.

But what waited had waited too long already. Setting her shoulders, holding her heart fast in her hands, Noni walked with Rabbit to the sleeping grave.

Noni wasn't fooled by the lush growth, the outrageous abundance of life that had seemingly flourished there for ages. Alaska was first and last a devourer. Whatever fell into Alaska's arms stayed there, and swiftly lost all its form and distinction as she covered it with her draping sleeves and heavy skirts. One season in Alaska looked like six anywhere else. And it had been far longer than a single season since this secret was hidden here, and this log dragged into place and camouflaged with moss and leaves.

Noni pulled her trowel from her pocket and dug from her knees in a position of petition and prayer that did not wait on an answer but found its own. Moss had joined hands with itself, deep in the dirt, and fought to keep her at bay, but she cut ruthlessly through its knotted fingers. In the shaded forest, the air was cool, the wind plucking and biting at her skin as if to worry her away from her work. By the time she found her prize, though, she was sweating, her face smudged, her fingernails caked with dirt.

Rabbit sat atop the log, her scuffed glass eyes gleaming as the first bone shone white from the dark earth. Noni rocked back on her heels, her gaze instinctively going to Beaver Woman. Beaver Woman's back was stiff, unbending, her long chestnut hair flowing down her back as she raised her face to the sun. She would not look on this end, would not acknowledge such a story.

It's only paper, Noni imagined Beaver Woman would say. Look where Ryska's fire still burns. This poor ash is only what is consumed. She is more than what ignites.

Noni saw the flames, but the bones still broke her. She dipped her finger in the dirt where she knew Ryska's skin and hair and clothes had disintegrated into the matter of life and drew lines of mud across her own cheeks.

I see you, Ryska.

Noni slowed her digging now, a careful excavation revealing one by one the huddled discard of Ryska's skeleton. She did not question who lay there. Who else would Rabbit bring her to see? Who else had she seen and heard and smelled rising from the floorboards of the cabin where Mary had told her Ryska's boyfriend used to bring her? What other ghost dogged her steps as she walked these arboreal mazes?

Little enough ceremony had accompanied the concealment of this sister of hers. She appeared to have been tossed in hurriedly, her limbs folding in on themselves so that she was nearly fetal in rest. Her jaw gaped, and Noni wondered if she had been crying out as she died or if this final expression of horror was only a late indignity of decay. She couldn't help cradling the bony skull, so child-like in its vulnerability, imagining she felt silken dark hair under her palm.

Noni lay down and curled up beside the grave, reaching down to thread the finger bones in her own hand.

So Mary-mother was Mary-the-bereaved. Noni had suspected, of course, when she'd first learned of Mary's loss. Everyone knew the statistics, how unlikely it was that any kidnapping victim would survive more than the first few hours. She knew, though, that Mary held out hope—if one could call it that—that her daughter had been trafficked or was being held in secret somewhere, that she could still be rescued, still be found.

The search for Ryska had defined Mary's entire existence as long as Noni had known her. Even now, she realized Mary played some bizarre long game thinking Noni's disappearance would somehow merit her Ryska's return.

But Ryska couldn't return. What did that make Mary? What became of a mother with no child?

Beaver Woman crouched in the underbrush, tracing out a message in the forest loam and fallen leaves that Noni couldn't see. Rabbit regarded Noni still, her whiskered face pleading silently.

So one ghost became guardian of another, Noni thought wearily. Little enough remained of her own identity, every scrap of memory hard-won and hard-held. She imagined the reason so many specters were pictured as faceless orbs of light or drifting curtains of light was because the spirits themselves had long since forgotten their shapes. She lifted her hand from Ryska's gentle grip and traced her own cheekbones, her chin. She still had a face. She still had a name.

She could carry them both a little longer, couldn't she?

But how much longer? And where was she carrying them?

The quiet glacier that had been building under her skin, growing colder and fiercer in its inexorable course toward destruction melted away beneath the glare of Ryska's empty eye sockets, leaving her all water.

Mary-mother, Mary-monster, eater of her flesh, cannibal of her soul, was so terribly hungry, and Noni lay here knowing Mary would never be filled again. Her empty belly would cramp forever. She had already starved to death and didn't know it, the empty husk of her body animated by a hope whose corpse stared at Noni from the dirt.

Noni had been waiting patiently, expectant on a signal from Beaver Woman to kill the cannibal and find her way upriver, just as the story said. But maybe the story wasn't hers, after all. Maybe the unseen creature who had lain Ryska in this grave had been the cannibal all along. Maybe Mary had been the maiden fighting against lovers and fools and enemies. Maybe the story was only a lie, and there was no power, no victory.

Noni pushed herself up, crossed her legs, returned Rabbit's steady gaze.

It would be more than cruel enough to leave Mary behind, she realized. What would become of the older woman with no child to tend, however grotesquely? Noni pictured Mary alone in the cabin, wandering in the woods, hands empty, eyes searching.

It was no small thing to kill a person. She might have killed a monster, an ogre, a beast, with little enough effort. A rush of fury and contempt would be enough to carry her through the act. She'd nearly done it before, though now that felt like something someone else had done while wearing her skin. She could hardly remember how the scissors had plunged into May's neck, how her hands had shaken with rage and resolve. It was a story she'd been telling herself, to remind her of who she'd been, who she could be again when the moment came.

Now the story seemed less fairytale than horror. She imagined killing Mary only to find a grieving mother rather than a snarling wendigo gasping out its last in her arms. Finding Ryska had resurrected the Mary Nelson Noni had long since buried. The fierce advocate, the staunch ally. The unfailing defender, the rallying inspiration, the relentless warrior. The friend.

Mary was terribly, terribly sick. And Noni couldn't kill her, not even to save herself. Not that saving herself was a sure thing to begin with. Ryska had thought to save herself, too, surely. And here she lay, wordlessly waiting on Noni to find a way to carry her out. If Noni could've given up on herself, she couldn't give up on Ryska. For Ryska's sake, if not her own, Noni had to find her way free. But not at the cost of Mary's life.

Tenderly Noni replaced the dirt and leaves that had formed the lid to Ryska's earthen coffin.

Rabbit and Beaver Woman trailed her as she retraced her steps to the cabin. She set the kettle on the woodstove for tea, feeling more solidly inside her own bones than she had in a long, long time. She took weird pleasure in the chattering percussion of her teeth, the shivering of goose-pimpled flesh in her damp clothes.

On the shelf beside the bed she spilled a few grains of dirt. Mary would be nearer to her daughter than she knew, the next time she slept beside Noni. It was the only grace Noni could offer her now.

Noni felt the strength of the earth wrapping around her ankles, holding her fast. She drew a deep breath. It was time to stop wandering.

YEAR SIX
Mary Nelson

Mary pushed back her short, iron-gray hair with a shaking hand. She'd come to hate her desk. Nothing good ever happened when she sat at the battered old wooden beast. Outside the window, a kaleidoscope of impossible colors moved across the twilight sky: fuchsia, magenta, violet, blue, the strange and wonderful pastels of the short winter days. The sun clung to its narrow track just above the horizon, where soon enough the mountains would again swallow it up. Mary wished she lived on the season's hours, like her ancestors had done, but she was bound to this farcical world and all its constructs and payments, payments, payments.

A stack of bills lay to her right, beside the empty vodka glass. That was another problem. The seal pup used to tease her that she drank too much, but Mary had assured her she only needed maintenance doses to get through the day. It wasn't as if she were ever actually drunk. Just functional. Now, though, the alcohol didn't even offer that hemming up of her raveled pieces that she'd come to rely on. Stitch after stitch fell out, and the vodka only made her thirsty.

Mary wasn't a typical political candidate, with deep pockets and trust funds and backdoor deals paying for her living expenses while she devoted herself to cameras and sound bites. She was the charity candidate, the one people voted for because it made them feel like a better person. She'd worked every day of her life since college—well, during college, too. Always ambitious, she'd been frugal with her earnings and diversified her meager savings as much as she could between retirements accounts and mutual funds. Since this campaign of her own started, though, she hadn't been working aside from the occasional consultation gig, and her cupboards were getting pretty bare.

She could try to get more work, but that was tricky too. Appearances were everything, and nobody wanted the desperate ticket. She needed to look confident, successful, unworried at all times. She could sell the house, but it wasn't as if she could find a cheaper place to live. Besides, this had been Ryska's home. Her bedroom was still in place, though Mary had long ago denied herself permission to go in there.

Not that Ryska had been living at home when she disappeared—not exactly, anyway. Mostly she'd lived with her boyfriend. But every few days she seemed to wind up at home, just for a night or two. At first Mary had played interrogator, demanding to know why Ryska was crying, where the bruises were hiding. Eventually she'd realized if she wanted her daughter to keep coming home, she'd better leave her in peace. So she would just brew a cup of hot tea, make her little rabbit a grilled cheese sandwich and some tomato soup, and they'd watch reruns on Netflix under piles of blankets till Ryska dragged her aching self upstairs to her childhood bedroom. Mary consoled herself with the knowledge that for a couple of days, her daughter was safe and sober. If that was all she could offer, so be it. One day, one day, Ryska would come home and not leave again. One day she would be strong. Until then, Mary would be strong for her.

Closing her eyes, Mary clung to the cross around her neck and pictured her daughter's room as she'd seen it last. A mess, of course. She laughed to herself a little weepily. That had to be one of the least realistic things about TV representations of the bedrooms of the lost. They were always so pristine, so clean. Ruffled bedskirts and pop posters neatly hanging on the walls. Mary admitted she'd gathered up the dirty dishes and the trash, but she'd left everything else just as it was. The unmade bed waiting for Ryska to crawl back under its sheets. The sweater thrown over the back of her desk chair. Half-packed boxes even Ryska had known there was no point in moving. A half-read romance novel waiting to be finished. A dusty bottle of hand lotion on the nightstand. The blinds still drawn where Mary knew Ryska had stood, watching the aurora borealis sing across the sky.

No, selling the house wasn't an option.

Home equity loan it would have to be, then. Mary hated the idea; she'd only just paid off the house three years earlier. She wasn't thrilled about the public knowing she'd gone begging, which is what it felt like, but she figured she could spin it as more evidence of her devotion to the people. She was the candidate who put her own house on the line for the chance to serve. Theoretically, she could keep it quiet, but she was a strong believer in transparency when it came to candidate finances. A politician was going to need to lie often enough as it was. Be honest about everything you can, especially money. People tended to be tetchy on the subject of corruption, as well they might, especially in Alaska. Personally, Mary found officials reluctant to disclose their finances downright irritating. It wasn't as if they hadn't been groomed for their positions all their lives, in most cases. Think ahead! If you had to do something dirty, then for Pete's sake, keep it off your own books. The public adored the unicorn concept of an honest politician. Give them some sparkle to believe in, and they'd be all over it.

She'd been a martinet on the subject with her seal pup, and it had paid off for the pup, too. Of course, the pup had struggled with some of Mary's rules more than others. She'd have been quite happy to put a few pairs of shoes on credit, but Mary had been iron on the subject. If the seal pup was going to help manage the nation's finances, she absolutely had to manage her own first. No debt outside of a home mortgage was the first rule. Now Mary was breaking that rule herself, and she needed cash to clean that up. Maintaining two households and all the travel had been more of a drain than she'd anticipated. Sometimes she was able to hide the expenses of caring for her pup in her campaign outlays, but she limited that as much as she could. The last thing she wanted to do was rouse any suspicions. Any hint of donation misuse was one of the quickest ways to lose voters.

Losing was not an option. Mary had made her peace long ago with the fact that she'd never be a poster girl, thought herself content with being the power behind the scenes. Now that she'd suddenly and unexpectedly been thrust into the role she'd never even allowed herself to dream of, she wasn't about to give it up. Nights she'd once spent lying awake picturing Ryska hurt, broke, frightened, she now spent plotting and planning her Washington maneuvers. Always she imagined Ryska there with her. It was impossible, surely, that she and the seal pup could make all these sacrifices, manage all these machinations, and still not find her. Ryska was out there. Somewhere, someone knew something. Mary had never been a gambler, but now she believed, absolutely, that this roll would be hers. She'd banked everything, even her soul.

God wouldn't ignore that. She was the widow who'd given her two mites, or the woman who offered her own son's last meal to the prophet in a time of famine. She was giving it all. God was a rewarder of the faithful. He would bring her Ryska back, just like He'd brought the woman's son back from the dead. You couldn't fly until you threw yourself into open air.

Mary refilled her glass, sipped the vodka thoughtfully. It was an affectation, maybe, not to drink it straight from the bottle, but it gave her some measure of deliberation. She would get the loan.

That decision made, she shoved the stack of bills back into the desk drawer and finished off her glass. Her pup was waiting.

As usual, she loaded up her car in the garage where no one could watch her. Suburbs bred bored observers in every window, and Juneau was more of a small town than a state capitol. With her frequent meetings with people all over the state, her travel elicited no curiosity these days, but she wasn't taking any chances. Even where there was no story, people loved to make them up. She wasn't going to provide them with any fuel.

Christmas had come and gone, but she had a gift for her seal pup all the same. She knew these long, dark days dragged on the pup's feeble spirit. Autumn had provided some distraction with the garden harvest. Mary had brought canning supplies and demonstrated the simple process to the pup. Now the shelves were lined with colorful jars and cheesecloth bags full of dried herbs and flowers. Together they'd gone hunting the meadows and woods for wild blueberry and raspberry brambles and filled jar after jar with preserves. They'd braved the fierce thorns of wild rosebushes to gather precious rosehips. Not only were they remarkably packed with vital nutrients, processing them was sufficiently laborious and time-intensive to occupy many of the pup's empty hours.

All that had been months ago. Mary had tried to teach the pup to knit, but she only ever created streamers of multi-colored wools, like giant scarves, that she draped over the walls. Mary didn't understand why she didn't have the slightest interest in actually creating something useful, like a hat or a sweater or even just a pair of socks. The pup seemed content with her never-ending rows, but the mindlessness of the rambling colors unnerved Mary. The longer they relied on each other, the further the pup retreated. That was how Mary saw it, and she didn't know how to stop it.

At least the pup wasn't spending every spare moment splayed out on the ground anymore. As far as Mary knew, anyhow. That stage had lasted longer than Mary cared to contemplate. She'd tamed her pup, all right, but even with rebellion replaced with docility, something feral crawled behind those dark eyes. If anything, Mary suspected the pup grew wilder, claws sheathed but lengthening and sharpening all the time. Comprehension flashed less and less.

Mary wondered just how sex traffickers did it. How could you keep a person in captivity for so long and still keep them human? But she supposed humanity wasn't a consideration for them, only performance. From what she'd read, they relied heavily on drugs to keep their merchandise malleable and simply disposed of them when they'd exceeded their shelf life. Ryska, she told herself, would not have met that end. Ryska was so much more than they'd imagined. Ryska would survive anything. Ryska was out there, waiting for her mother to bring her home. And bring her home she would.

Today, though, she needed to tend to her seal pup. She was hoping her gift would provoke the pup to curiosity, to delight, to adventure, even. A pair of snowshoes would make the snow-and-ice-packed muskeg easily traversable. The pup had grown too sedentary, and winter too easily became a cage. Snowshoes would be the key that would unlock her.

Mary had just hit the garage door opener when her phone rang. She put the car back in park and looked at the caller ID.

Izak. The fisherman. He must have returned to shore, no longer able to find respite in the succor and savagery of the sea. Sighing heavily, she answered the phone. Just like the seal pup's parents, her lover and his loss were also her cross to bear.

A few moments later, she pressed the *end* button with a shaking finger and rested her head against the steering wheel. Damn, damn, and double-damn.

One of the members of the busted sex-trafficking ring that she'd seen in the news last week had apparently confessed to the kidnapping of Alaska Senator-Elect Noni Begay. A ruse, of course, perhaps a desperate ploy to win a better plea bargain or just the ravings of some drug-addled madman, but how could she possibly explain knowing that? She had to be relieved, had to be overjoyed, had to be fraught with anxiety and terror and anticipation as she waited along with everyone else to learn what had become of the victim.

The cormorants and coyotes would be circling any moment now. No chance of leaving town until she'd made all the rounds, and maybe not even then. Panic clawed at her insides. It took three tries to get the seatbelt off. She flung herself out of the car before dropping to her knees in a silent howl, unwilling even now to unleash her emotions from the fierce control she always maintained over them. She knew, knew too well, that a mad dog once freed could only be brought back to the cage lifeless.

Slowly, deliberately, she dragged herself off the cold concrete, scraped her hair back with careful hands, settled her face back into its usual inscrutable mask that fools were so inclined to read as serene. How long, she wondered, would it take the cormorants to verify the suspect's claims and discover that they were purest fantasy?

This would mean an immediate round of interviews and public appearances. That would have been true in any circumstance, but especially as a senatorial candidate, her presence was vital. Not to mention how strange it would have looked had she been absent.

There was nothing to worry about, she told herself sternly. The seal pup would be fine. There were plenty of canned goods and foodstuffs. Even with her hobbled gait, she was perfectly capable of bringing in wood, although Mary always did the chopping when she was there. That was the real worry. The seal pup could probably manage if she had to, but Mary knew she wasn't strong. She wouldn't know to conserve her supplies, and she wouldn't have any idea when the absence would end. Mary usually varied the amount of time between her visits, just to keep from attracting attention, but never by more than three or four days. She was already at the end of that extension now. She'd stacked extra wood under the tap out back, because a storm could rise up at any time, but miraculously, she'd always made it through in the past. She had to believe that there would be enough this time, too.

The pup was smart. The pup wouldn't panic. She was a good girl. She would manage. She knew Mary would never leave her.

For now, Mary had to focus on maintaining appearances here. The faster she could meet these obligations, the sooner she could get to her pup. So what would she have done if this story were true? If she didn't know where the pup was, what would be her first move?

The Begays, of course. She needed to call the pup's parents. She closed the garage door behind her as she walked back into her kitchen, started the kettle for tea, and hit dial on the Begays' name in her phone contacts.

Mrs. Begay's voice broke over Mary's ears like a river in the spring thaw breaking over boulders. All that roaring, all that speed, all that power. Soon enough, Mary knew, that energy would be exhausted when the truth came out, when this terrible hope withered back to blackened rot. She had been down that road many times herself. How many false leads, how many times had she waited anxiously after the arrest of yet another drug dealer, yet another sex offender, yet another murderer? Nothing, she decided, tasted so acrid on the tongue as a mother's hope that finally, she would have a body to bury. And for even that hope to die, again and again? It was too much to bear.

So for now, she allowed Mrs. Begay to run unchecked. There was always time enough for despair. No need to point out all the possibilities to the woman now.

They agreed that Mary would appear with them at the press conference. The cormorants weren't thrilled about them talking to the media, but Mary agreed with the pup's parents that it was best to feed the coyotes early. And maybe, she'd concurred, maybe the coyotes could help get to the bottom of the man's story that much more quickly. She'd allowed Mrs. Begay to assume that she meant confirming it and not disproving it.

Two weeks.

Two weeks blinking in the glare of media lights and constant public scrutiny, two weeks of looking grimly hopeful and propping up all the family and friends who had re-emerged with all their pretty tears and fanciful memories. Amazing how dear and precious the missing became when they only required a few minutes in front of a camera and a social media post or two once every other year. Grief lent such a pretty sheen—who didn't want to be a mourner? Please, give me some sad faces, retweet me, like my carefully morose photos and curated memories. People felt so much more important when they could lay claim to other people's sympathies.

How Mary despised them. Not the pup's parents, or even her well-meaning but aggravating former lover, of course. Their torment was real, visceral, haunting in its rigid containment. No, it was the others—the sorority sisters, the cousins, the coworkers, the baristas—who couldn't wait to trot out their connections and claim their own vicarious victimhood. And everybody had to wear a fucking braid, even the blondes.

She bought vodka by the six-pack, ostensibly for the discount, but really in case anyone was tracking how many times she stopped by the liquor store. She knew you could buy wine online and have it delivered; was that an option for vodka, too? Maybe she should look into it. It wouldn't do to have people speculating that she was just another Injun enslaved to firewater. People might elect a stereotype with glee, but no one would elect a caricature.

She dreaded the sight of her own bed. Vodka had long ago ceased to help her sleep, and now she spent each night staring into the darkness, sweating her hair damp even while her feet turned to blocks of ice. Perhaps she could have persuaded herself that all was well, had not a rare and bitter deep freeze settled over the region, sending temperatures plunging well below zero. The cabin was far from weathertight, although she'd made many improvements to the interior. She thought of the seal pup forced to brave the frigid, howling winds to reach the outhouse, only to return to a still-cold bed.

During the summer months, Mary had hauled plenty of logs into the copse near the cabin, but they still needed to be chopped. Had the seal pup tried to chop the wood herself? That was a nonsensical thought, Mary knew; the sharpest implement she had was a hand trowel. What if she'd injured herself? Or fallen sick in the cold temperatures? Last year she'd only stopped that mad earth-listening after she'd gotten soaked through in the spring and begun coughing her lungs up. Mary had had to fake an illness of her own to get antibiotics for her, and still it had taken weeks for her to regain her strength. Pneumonia, maybe. At any rate, Mary felt it had weakened the pup. She couldn't afford another illness. But what if she was sick already, out there all alone?

It had only taken a few days for the cormorants to realize that they were being had by their suspect, but the coyotes required regular attention for some time after that. As had the Begays. Mary had been with them, at their home, when the detective had called.

She'd known, her eyes fixed on Mr. Begay as he held the phone to his ear. Though scarcely a muscle moved, his face had somehow crumbled like volcanic ash under the rain. It had surprised her, shocked her almost, how badly it hurt to watch. The father's stoic anguish cut her more deeply than the mother's wails. She had held Mrs. Begay as she curled into herself, said all the same useless things stupid people had said to her, because as it turned out, there was nothing else to say.

Even now, she tasted that ash on her tongue. She did not think she would ever rinse it away. It was as if, before her eyes, the father had become a corpse, a spiritless skin forced to keep jerking through life day to day.

But their agony would not last forever, she reminded herself. Their daughter was not dead. They would hold her again. They would hear her voice again. They would have their spirits restored.

Just like she would. When Ryska came home. When Ryska came home.

Today, though, she needed to get to her seal pup. At last the pressure had eased.

She stopped by a gas station like some ridiculous tourist and paid an outrageous amount for a small bundle of firewood that she could take in on the snowmobile. Luckily she wasn't the glamorous sort that a clerk might recognize from television. Just another round little old lady. Fifty-six wasn't that old, but she felt closer to seventy-six these days. She wanted to be able to build a fire the moment she arrived. This time she would chop wood till her shoulders screamed and her palms burned. Never again would she worry that her pup was cold out there, cold like Ryska might be.

Even with all her scarves and hat and handwarmers and footwarmers and thick parka, Mary felt half-frozen by the time she finally reached the cabin. The wind bit fiercely at her fingers as she worked the lock. The deep freeze, so atypical for this part of Alaska, still hadn't lifted.

As she slipped in and closed the door behind her as quickly as she could, her gaze immediately sought the dim lantern light burning in the corner. Dear Mother of God, the cabin was so cold. The seal pup was tucked up in the corner of the bed, covered in blankets, pillows a wall around her, the lantern a feeble warmth for her outstretched hands.

Those dark eyes, that had frightened her with their feral light just a few weeks ago, now gazed back dull and listless.

Mary didn't hesitate. She crossed the room in three strides, swinging the bundle of firewood off her back and building a fire in the wood stove in just a couple of minutes. As the tiny flames licked up the wood and flung out their blazing tongues, the seal pup came scampering off the bed, blankets still drawn tightly around her, and settled on the bricks in front of the stove, eagerly bathing her pale face in its light.

Lowering herself to the ground behind the pup, Mary wrapped her own body tightly around the thin trembling frame that huddled in quilts, squeezing her with all her strength. The pup seized Mary's forearms in her hands and squeezed back, a desperate, pathetic gesture of love and terror, hope and despair. Mary rocked her seal pup in her arms as her own tears broke free without warning, and she stifled the wails she could not silence against the cotton fabric.

How much longer would she have to wait? Seventeen people had been arrested in that sex-trafficking bust, and that was only one of many in the sixteen years since Ryska had disappeared. Mary knew that no one lasted that long in the business, but surely, in all that time, someone would have seen her. Someone would have known what became of her. But none of those arrests had led to any sign of her little rabbit. What was she searching for, after all? For her daughter? Or only for her bones?

Had Ryska succumbed to the cold long ago, without her own mother even knowing she had left the earth? Had anyone held her as she held the seal pup now? Had anyone comforted her? Or had it all been cold and fear and awful until the end?

Mary thought of the seal pup, waiting and waiting and waiting as the cold grew fiercer. Had Ryska waited, in that same terrible anticipation of hope, looking and listening for her mother's steps, steps that never came?

I'm coming, Ryska. She choked on her sobs. *I'm coming. I'm coming. Don't give up. Look for the light. I am coming.*

By the time she'd recovered her breath and her mind cleared, she'd wasted precious minutes of warmth and light. She untangled herself from the pup's embrace to bundle back up and go start chopping wood, but the pup cried out and clutched her tighter. The pup's terror cut at Mary's heart, but soon enough the pup would realize that she wasn't leaving. Gently she detached the pup's claw-like hands and wrapped herself up against the cold. As petrified as the little creature clearly was of being abandoned again, she wasn't about to leave the warmth of the wood stove.

Dangerous, this sort of cold. Mary would have to limit her time out, chopping in short bursts and coming back in to warm up frequently. Her arthritis was not any too fond of the temperatures, either, but Mary just washed a couple ibuprofen down with vodka and went out again and again. Fortunately, the long freeze lifted after two more days, which made the task much more pleasant. Still, Mary chopped wood all five days that she stayed at the cabin, determined that her pup would never be cold like that again.

Five days was longer than she would normally have stayed, but there was no help for it. She could plead emotional exhaustion after the events of the last two weeks, so she wasn't too worried about making her excuses on that score. She'd had to make several trips back and forth on the snowmobile to her car to collect all the supplies she'd brought this time. Fortunately, her worst fear, that the pup would have fallen ill again, hadn't come true. She'd agonized over whether she should leave medicines at the cabin in case of another emergency, but the pup's good health had made up her mind for her. The fear that, after all this time, the pup might fall prey to despair and end her own life, nagged at her. Bottles of pills might prove too strong a temptation. The pup had made it through this crisis whole and hale. Mary would take her chances and return the medicines in her car back to her house in town.

Teas and herbs and supplements would keep the pup feeling well enough. She had pineapple juice and honey and marshmallows in case of a sore throat, Mary reassured herself. No need to allow her own personal sense of panic to further endanger the pup by leaving pills lying about. After all, they'd made it this long. They could make it to the end.

Hale and whole wasn't the same as untroubled, though. The bleakness in the pup's eyes only lifted when it was replaced by terror every time she thought Mary was leaving again. The poor creature had no idea what had happened in Juneau, of course. She had no way of understanding that Mary had no choice, that her absence had been absolute necessity rather than desire. So she had no way of knowing that Mary wouldn't again leave her alone for so long, that she'd soon be back just as she always had been before.

The long-delayed gift of the snowshoes proved disappointing. Though the pup buckled her boots in with alacrity and happily accompanied Mary as they tromped across the frozen muskeg and through the quiet forest, the joy in her face was pinched with continual anxiety. The crunch of snow and ice under their feet rattled through the pristine air, accenting the severity of their solitude. Ravens watched, solemn-eyed, and occasionally a moose shifted out of sight round the trees ahead. Mary hoped that in her absence, the pup would come walk these same paths and feel close to her until she returned.

That parting was the bitterest of Mary's life.

Though the roar of the snowmobile quickly drowned out the piteous cries echoing from behind the cabin door, Mary swore she could hear them still, reverberating against her ears all the long drive back to Juneau. In bed that night, and for many nights after, she jerked awake with a guttural wail of her own, reaching for the pup's clutching hands just as they vanished into the snow. When she slept, she dreamed of cold, shaking fingers wrapped in her own that turned to bone as she chafed them warm.

YEAR SIX
Noni Begay

It hadn't been so easy to stop wandering, after all. Just as Noni returned to her body, it betrayed her. Maybe she'd breathed in some kind of bacteria, lying beside Ryska's grave in the fetid, mushroom-garlanded earth. Maybe her system had been too weak to suffer the cold and damp in the rain-soaked dirt and leaves. At any rate, she'd been fever-bound in bed for days.

Somewhere in there Mary had shown up and tended her as sweetly and tenderly as any mother would tend a sick child. Noni had vague memories of cool cloths and warm soup and soft hands and fluffy blankets. Being sick wasn't the convenient literary device Russian novels and Victorian romances made it out to be. No ghostly apparitions visited her, no spirits imparted sacred wisdom, no dark truths made it out to the light of fever-dreams. She sweated, and ached, and slept, and finally woke up tired of the taste of soup and the smell of her own skin.

Mary stood at the woodstove with her back to Noni. Her shoulders were bent, her black and iron-grey hair unkempt. She wasn't Mary-mother, or even Mary-monster, anymore. She was simply Mary Nelson, the woman Noni knew best in the world. Fighting fatigue, Noni pushed herself to a sitting position, leaned back against the wooden wall of the cabin.

Mary must have sensed the motion, because she turned. The anxiety carved into her face re-sorted itself into pleasure when she saw Noni alert and upright.

She hurried across the room to sit beside Noni on the bed and cup her cheek in her palm, checking her temperature.

Despite herself, Noni tucked her head into Mary's palm, taking brief solace from the affection. There was something holy about carrying a grief for someone who didn't know it existed yet. Noni didn't even consider the possibility of leading Mary out to the woods to reveal what she'd found there. What a terrible cruelty that would be. And instinctively, Noni understood whatever Mary thought to accomplish by keeping her here would be undone by that discovery. Far from setting her free, Noni suspected the truth might bury them both.

Unexpectedly, a strong sense of protectiveness suffused her as she looked into the older woman's face, with its falling curtains of sorrows and cynicism, its bleak black gaze devoid of words. In her strange way, Mary had protected and cared for Noni more closely, more devoutly, than anyone else in Noni's life. Even her parents had not shared this sort of single-minded, solitary existence with her. Noni couldn't imagine how Mary was functioning in the outside world. Maybe she wasn't functioning at all. Maybe she'd abandoned all effort at life outside of what she shared here with Noni.

Noni didn't think so, though. She felt certain that if Mary weren't somehow anchored in the outside world, she'd spend every moment in this cabin with her. She must still be working, must be fighting to accomplish something out there. In all the time Noni had known her, Mary's passions had been singular. They'd shared the conviction that almost anything was justified to win the election, because without that, they had no hope of affecting real change. Winning was everything. And they needed to win because so many had lost. So many *were* lost.

Whatever Mary did when she left the cabin, she was still fighting to win. Noni knew that incontrovertibly.

And yet, she'd already lost everything and didn't know it yet. Other people might think that was wildly optimistic and irrational of Mary. Law enforcement and the public had long ago acknowledged that Ryska was certainly dead by now, even if she remained officially a missing person. All the flyers bearing her face and name had long since faded and been torn down and thrown away. No search parties marched across the muskeg for her.

But a mother couldn't stop looking for her child. A mother believed, with her heart and mind and belly and empty arms, her child lived. Her child waited to be found. A mother wasn't permitted the grace of mourning while her child had no grave, no marker, no end to her story. If her child had no rest, then neither did she. A mother was allowed no relief while her child was forced to walk the twilight of not-dead and not-alive.

Noni didn't know if ending that torturous existence would be a mercy or a cruelty. Mary would have to find a way to learn herself as the mother bereaved instead of the mother searching. She shuttered her own gaze, hoping no glint of the truth gleamed there. Mary only patted her head and retrieved a box of crackers to tempt her with.

Actually, Noni was starving, so she finished off almost the entire box along with the steaming cup of sweet milky tea Mary made her. Facing Mary's loss made her acutely aware of the loss her own parents must suffer. Noni had tried to keep thoughts of home and family at bay since those early weeks that now seemed the foggiest of dreams. Now, as she emerged from her fever, she felt too as if she emerged from a twilight existence of her own. Thoughts of home, of Izak, of her mother and father, crowded insistently, flooding her eyes with hot, unexpected tears.

Hastily she wiped them away before Mary could see them and wonder. Her position here, her chance of escape, relied on Mary taking her acquiescence, even her happiness, for granted. She had no idea how she was going to get away from here without overpowering her captor, but her resolve had never been fiercer. She would find a way. For now, she would wait, and watch, and plan.

Longing for home, for her mother's embrace, her father's warm gaze, swelled painfully inside her. Izak had surely long since forgotten her. She laughed weepily under her breath to think what a good first-date story she must be, the tragic backstory for a handsome fisherman on the make. If he still said her name at all. Self-pity raised its head, eager for a bit of food, but she quashed it. The truth was, he'd been a far better boyfriend than she'd been a girlfriend. Partner was too generous a term for the meager role she'd allowed him in her life. He hadn't been exactly camera-ready, a little too rough around the edges, a little too dark-skinned for the votes she needed to win. So she'd kept him conveniently in her pocket for occasional companionship and little else. If her disappearance had bettered his chances on the dating market, she figured he deserved it.

Mom and Dad, though…they'd never have been able to relegate her to a story they told over dinner. They hadn't had one of those relationships she knew some of her peers had, where they called each other every day, had Sunday dinner every week, but they hadn't needed to. Her parents supported and believed in her absolutely. She thought of her mother waking up every morning the same way Mary did, lying in the hot sheets with open eyes as the reality of her missing daughter washed over her, new and awful every time. She thought of her father, the fixer who couldn't fix this, retreating to his garage and his shop, looking for broken things he could put back together.

Again she pushed thoughts of her parents away, but this time she didn't try to bury them deep inside herself. She built a room in her head where she could keep them, allow herself to say their names and remember their faces. If she was going to find a way home, she had to find the way back to herself first. Beaver Woman and Rabbit had helped her create a world she could navigate here without fear and pain, but it was like all spirit worlds: dangerous for those who still walked in flesh. Its allure beckoned, promised safety and magic, a refuge from the stark horrors of the day. Getting lost on its timeless paths was a luxury she could no longer afford. From now on, Beaver Woman and Rabbit would have to follow Noni, not the other way around.

Even as Noni rededicated herself to escape, she missed Mary more each time she left. Maybe, she told herself, it was simple psychology. As she invested more and more heavily in the "real" world, it made sense she'd grow increasingly attached to the only human relationship she still had. She struggled continually to keep both drives separate, her longing to see Mary again and her determination to leave the woman and this confinement behind forever.

Mary's long, strange absence during the coldest days of winter only intensified these warring inclinations. Nightmarish possibilities tormented Noni as she huddled under the blankets in painful cold. As incredible as it seemed that Mary might be subject to mortality after all, maybe she was dead. Maybe she would never return. Maybe Noni would freeze to death, alone and hungry and forgotten. Snow heaped in piles as far as Noni could see. Leaving the cabin, in these temperatures and with no clear sense of where to go, would bring certain death. But clutching her own knees under the covers with only Rabbit and Beaver Woman for warmth, waiting for death to reach her, was an equally awful proposition. By the time Mary at last returned, bringing fire and food with her, Noni felt half-mad with fear and her own unbearable dependence. When she wrapped herself around the older woman in a frenzy of love and terror, she wanted equally to frame Mary's face tenderly in her hands and to smash it like a clay bowl.

Noni wasn't the only one fighting irrational urges. She was surprised when Mary brought reams and reams of yarn and brightly colored knitting needles and taught Noni how to knit. Although so much time had passed—she didn't know how much, but it had to have been years, didn't it?—she'd have thought her failed attempt with the scissors would have convinced Mary she could never be trusted with a potential weapon. But Mary must have wanted to believe as much as Noni did that something in their strange little family was real, after all.

Even so, words hadn't returned to their world. The Books were gone for good, it seemed. Sometimes Noni indulged in reminiscing the sounds and shapes of those stories, the way the notes dropping from Mary's lips had made symphony with the images on the pages, how she'd seen Star-People and cannibals and maidens and rivers and moon-lovers move effortlessly from paper to life.

She didn't need them anymore, Noni told herself. She was the author of her own book. Fairytales were for children under the dominion of adults, children who dreamed of magic and power that would make sense of the world and set them free. Noni's power breathed under her own skin. She was the magic she sought. This trap she was in was only an illusion, a paltry bewitchment whose sorcery could not stand against her own.

Like any good witch, she resolved to use Mary's own elements against her.

Escaping from this remote cabin and making it to civilization would be no small matter. Timing would be tricky. The growing seasons were warmer, but the ground was swampy, difficult for Noni to navigate with her bent legs. Every step landed differently, begging a twisted ankle or torn knee, injuries she could ill afford. And the dense growth was deceptive, confusing the eyes and all sense of direction.

It would be easy enough to follow the tracks of Mary's ATV back to whatever road she'd come in on, but Mary was canny enough to come from a variety of directions. A lifetime in this state had taught Noni how narrow the gap was between death and survival. She couldn't afford a single wasted step or hour once she left the safety of the cabin for good.

So she began a campaign of reconnaissance. Mary's returns were random, impossible to predict, so venturing too far was its own risk. All the while she was exploring, Noni's heart pounded, her hands shook. Her throat was dry, and her breath hitched and rasped unevenly. She'd have no explanation if Mary's ATV came roaring up the track she was on. No explanation that wouldn't leave the truth bare to Mary's gaze. Maybe Mary's madness left her a little gullible in her longing to accept Noni's submissiveness at face value, but she was no fool. And the continual throbbing ache in Noni's knees wouldn't let her forget the consequences of betrayal.

The first few times, she barely made it yards away before she hobbled hastily back, gulping air and tears and terror. But day by day, she forced herself to go farther and farther, following one track at a time back to the narrow dirt road that was itself hardly more than track.

And so Mary's gift of knitting needles and yarn became the amulet Noni needed to break the witch's hold. Noni knitted long narrow strips of color and hung them on the walls, a map drawn out in plain sight. She didn't trust herself any more than she trusted Mary. She knew how easily she might slip away, might drift back into the spirit realm where Beaver Woman and Rabbit waited for her. So she left the navigation on the walls, a road she could feel as well as see.

When she woke in the twilight grey of summer night, her eyes clung to the colors cobwebbed on the walls, promise of a way out. Spatial relations had never been a strong point of hers. She'd relied on GPS to get her anywhere she needed to go. Rather than trust her innate sense of distance, she decided at last the only way to be sure was simply to count. As she followed the worn tracks of Mary's ATV, she counted every step, driving a stick into the ground, well-camouflaged by weeds, every twenty-five paces.

So her map didn't just show direction, it showed distance, too. Noni knew it probably only reflected the actual topography she attempted to preserve in the loosest of senses, but it would supply what she needed most: a starting point.

Between her own dread of being caught, the slow pace necessitated by her twisted legs, and Mary's visits, finishing the map took forever. Six tracks shone out from the cabin like the rays of a sunset. She didn't know what geography lay behind the cabin, but it must offer no passable countryside at all. The trees were too thick for her to make out the horizon, but perhaps mountains stood that way, or one of the many nameless lakes surrounded only by swamp. At any rate, she was sure that direction offered no chance of escape. The only way out would be the way Mary came in.

That was only the first of her considerations, though. Once on the road, which way should she go? How many miles would she have to walk before she reached salvation?

She'd lost her wariness of people. Once she'd been well aware of the statistics in Alaska regarding violence against women—how dramatically higher odds were here of being murdered, raped, or abducted, despite the significantly smaller population—but none of that seemed real now. She might once have been leery of approaching some sagging shack in the woods, might have never imagined flagging down a stranger's car, but now she wouldn't hesitate. All she needed was to reach one person.

Even that was hardly guaranteed here, though. Even if she did find some kind of dwelling, odds were better than even it was only a hunting cabin or summer residence. And she had decided to wait for frozen ground to set out.

She simply couldn't travel fast enough to stand a chance while the ground was soft and the underbrush thick. Once she made it to the dirt road, she'd have a chance, but even the shortest track Mary took through the muskeg and the woods to the cabin was at least three miles long. If she heard the rumble of the ATV while she was out there, Noni would have to make her way back to the cabin and concoct a likely story for her absence, rather than risk Mary finding her and rendering her incapable of ever escaping.

Her only option was to leave as soon as Mary did. Sometimes Mary would circle back to check on her, but that happened rarely these days. Mary's paranoia was fading. Noni had to wait on a trifecta of happenstance: ground frost-frozen but not icy, good weather likely to hold, and Mary's departure. Too long, and snow might conceal all roads till spring. Too soon, and all would be lost. Even now, the thought of being discovered sent terror unspooling maniacally through her veins.

She saw the map unwinding in her dreams as she slept, a brilliant ribbon of verdant green over the grey-brown earth, guiding past every peril to safety. Rabbit and Beaver Woman followed at her heels, trusting her to know the way. Numbers pattered in the background of every thought, counting step after step in careful compulsion.

Waking, her neuroses grew ever stronger. Every day, the tension between the ghastly horror of being caught and the desperate, clawing, craving to escape tightened. Sometimes she couldn't tell if she delayed because conditions weren't yet right or because she was a coward. Other times she had to force herself to remain while every cell in her body screamed at her to run, to run now, regardless of any hope of success or certainty of failure.

But the season was turning. Every morning when she awoke, more leaves carpeted the ground. Her garden drowsed more and more, reluctant to rise with the sun. The muskeg grew sluggish. Psychedelic mushrooms, almost too fantastically painted to be real, sprouted everywhere beneath weeping reeds. Cranberries peeped scarlet, the last bounty of the year before the long dark winter imposed its cruel dearth. White crystallized flowers bloomed in the corners of the windows. The fear in Noni's belly grew fat and sleepy, preparing to hibernate and give courage its day.

Soon the snows would fall. Almost time to tell Mary goodbye.

Beaver Woman gathered her skirts.

AFTER THE ELECTION
Mary Nelson

She lost.

A cacophony of small sounds shattered against her ears, and she fought not to flinch. Chairs scraping over the hardwood floors, champagne glasses being abruptly set back on tabletops, indrawn breaths, stifled groans, the rustling of suits and dresses as people shifted awkwardly. Even the air trembled in an agony of relief and remorse.

But Mary Nelson was a professional to her core. She'd lost everything else in life, she'd allowed herself to be trotted around and remade in the image of whatever was likeliest, but she'd never sacrificed her dignity, and she wasn't about to start now. One hard breath, and then she had the microphone in her hand and the crowd back in the palm of her hand.

She'd prepared for either contingency, of course. Only a fool wouldn't have. And this race had been close from start to finish. There was a reason her supporters already had champagne in their glasses. A recount was inevitable with numbers this tight, but Mary knew that was only a formality the man who now filled her old role would insist on for appearance's sake. Grace, dignity, and hope— those were her signal message in this goodbye to the stage.

She was done.

Politics had been her first and last love, but politics failed her utterly in the end. She'd never been the idealist her little seal pup had been, but she'd been a true believer in the nitty-gritty, back room, back door, backstabbing machinations that she'd been convinced could change the world after all. Now, after serving the machine her entire life, she realized the machine only served itself. A closed loop, self-perpetuation was its only purpose. All her contacts, all her networking, all her knowledge of the system, and still her little rabbit was seventeen years gone. Without a trace.

Small sounds became loud sounds as her speech came to a close. Chairs clattered as everyone rose, clapping and cheering as if they hadn't all just lost. And really, Mary supposed, they hadn't. A small adjustment, a new seating chart, perhaps, some different palms to grease, but that was about the sum of it. Mary put in her time, nodding and smiling, shaking hands and accepting hugs, playing the role of the wise old native woman, content and accepting, one more time.

For a candidate who intended to continue on in the world of politics, whether as a public figure or a behind-the-scenes player, losing an election was hardly the end of the road, but Mary had no intention of making a graceful exit. This wasn't her world anymore. It hadn't been for a very long time. Let them talk. Let them wonder. It would be no matter to her. This night was her last hurrah.

Crushing disappointment swelled behind her eyes, threatening to blind her, swamp her with darkness. When she escaped the ballroom, she would let it cover her in its icy waves. For now, she had a room to navigate. Mary lifted her chin, set her shoulders, cloaked herself with the courage of countless women who had borne up before her. No one in this room would see her cry.

But by the time she made it home, the tears turned to salt on her tongue. She slipped out of her heels and unzipped her dress, letting it fall to the floor. Aimlessly, she wandered from room to room in her slip without turning on the lights. Black night pressed against the windows, peering in at her with sympathetic eyes. Her own gaze ping-ponged from one item to another, finding no place to rest. How much of it would she bother to pack?

Bleakly she wished that the aurora would gleam through the glass, but the night was cloudy. Here the clouds never seemed to abate.

She found herself standing outside Ryska's room. Softly she turned the knob, pushed the door open. Musty air assailed her nose. It had stopped smelling like Ryska so long ago.

"I'm sorry," she whispered, but her words fell stony to the carpeted floor. Not even a ghost answered her. Slowly she spun, her mind making sense of every shadow. This wasn't a bedroom. It was a museum exhibit.

All the plans for Washington…she shoved a fist against her mouth, but she didn't think she could make a sound if she wanted to. She'd been ready to save so many. Pride, she knew. Pride was her downfall. She'd thought her grief so much greater than that of all the other mothers, her rage blacker, her will fiercer.

But how could Ryska not be home? How could she have sacrificed so much, dared so much, to no end at all? And now? Now everything would proceed as it always had. No voice in Washington would recite the names of the missing. The cormorants and the coyotes would scatter and regroup around some other, fresher kill. Girls would become ghosts, one after another, haunting the blind and the deaf and the stony-hearted.

Feeling as though she had aged a thousand years, Mary crept back out of her daughter's room and closed the door behind her. She walked into her own bedroom and lay down on top of the covers, staring up at the ceiling as she shimmied out of her pantyhose. The last of her energy spent, she lay too tired to sleep. Sleep meant dreams, and dreams she could no longer afford. She wondered if the one-eyed Star-People looked down at her, above the billowing clouds, if they looked on Ryska too. Why would no one tell her where she was?

She would sell the house. Once it had seemed impossible, to abandon the house where her daughter's height was still marked on the kitchen doorjamb. Now she only wished she could burn it down instead. But if she were going to disappear, to retreat from this awful plastic world with its awful plastic people, she would have to discharge all her debts first. Truth was, she was drowning beneath the weight of this house and its equity loan anyway. What had been home was only a cage now, a prison of fear and loss and memory.

Mary gazed and gazed, until the darkness crashing against her carried her out into sleep after all. But she did not dream.

The next day, her phone rang and rang until she turned it off. She emailed a realtor she knew, setting up an appointment for a pre-contract inspection and instructing the agent that she would only be available for communication via email. She was done with these voices clamoring, clamoring all the time. Did no one listen anymore? Everyone lived on broadcast power. Every thought, every feeling they had, screamed at the world through tweets and posts, t-shirts and bumper stickers. Everything people touched, they painted with their own image. Tree trunks scratched with initials, bridges and train cars decked with gang signs, bathroom walls adorned with the most boring profanities. Even when people had nothing to say, still they festooned the world with their vapidity.

Mary remembered the year the seal pup had spent listening, cleaving to the earth, clasped around trees. Perhaps the pup had been right. Mary wondered what the pup had heard. Mary couldn't hear anything anymore. Sounds bounced around her ears like hard plastic shapes in one of the puzzle pails toddlers used to learn their circles and squares and triangles. When she concentrated, she could still find the match, could still summon the pre-programmed response the speaker expected, but comprehension was lost to her.

On a whim, Mary dropped the cardboard box she'd been unfolding and walked into the backyard. A grey November sky, shot through with pink and lavender, glowered at her. Mary drew her fleece robe tighter around the slip she still wore and dropped to her belly. Stiff, icy grass crunched beneath her. She turned her head, pressing her cheek to the ground and allowed the cold to seep deep into her bones.

A frigid breeze swept over her, ruffling her uncombed hair. She spread her fingers, spread her palms. With all her being, she strained, listening. Praying for a voice she could fathom. But the tongue of the wind was unfamiliar, and the earth did not speak at all.

She lay there a long time anyway, wondering if she would lie there long enough to become ice herself. But even the dead inside are driven to preserve the outside. Stiffly she pushed herself up at last, shivering as she hobbled back into the house on aching feet. Back to packing, then. Her seal pup needed her, anyway. Despair was a luxury of the selfish. She had work to do.

Packing and cleaning were a drudgery, but then, so was breathing. Mary worked methodically, her mind far removed from the mechanics of her muscles. She remembered this sensation well. It had lasted for weeks after she'd lost Ryska. That certainty that if she stopped moving, she might never start again. In the beginning, at least, she'd been able to lie to herself, convince herself that her ceaseless motion served some purpose. She'd driven up and down the city streets, eyes training for a familiar silhouette. She'd knocked on the door of every flophouse where she'd ever picked her little rabbit up. She called hospitals and shelters night after night. She'd driven out to the cabin property and searched and searched through the woods and the swamp, calling her daughter's name until her throat was hoarse.

Hope had been so high and sharp in those days. She'd fallen asleep, clutching it to her breast like a blade, and woken with it pricking at her throat. She'd clung to it, no matter how deeply it cut, certain that if she did all the right things, she could bring Ryska home. Her Ryska wasn't some missing Native girl. She wasn't a faded missing poster, a discarded junkie, a forgotten name on the news, a law passed in tribute, an icon of the lost. Ryska was her daughter, and she would bring her home. She would do all the right things.

But Mary had never found the right things. Everything she did came back to her empty.

The human spirit was a despicable thing, she'd learned. Unsinkable. Intent on its own persistence. Well-meaning friends and colleagues had urged her to bury herself in work, and to her own disgust, she'd succeeded. Not enough that her solitary hours weren't consumed with thoughts of Ryska cold, alone, hurting, afraid, but enough that she occasionally caught herself looking forward to a dessert or engrossed in a meeting. Enough that she hated herself for doing all the stupid things that people considered living—buying new clothes or clipping coupons or designing ad campaigns—while her daughter remained in limbo.

People grew tired of her grief with stunning swiftness. Pity is so only chic for so long, and then it is exhausting. They needed her to get on with her life so they could stop acknowledging how impossible that was.

And then she'd met her seal pup. Mary had discounted her at first, like everyone did. Too pretty, all her edges soft and rounded, her eyes full of dreams. Mary understood why the party wanted her rising on their tickets, and she thought they were right. Well-spoken, lovely, and brown-skinned, the pup had checked all the boxes for a party beset with scandals and liabilities. But the pup had been cannier than them all, knowing their assumptions all the time and more than willing to use them to her own advantage. More than clever, the pup was brilliant and passionate in an idealistic sense Mary could only pretend at.

Before she'd realized what was happening, Mary had fallen for the pup with the fierce, all-consuming, unfailing devotion of a mother for a child. Alliance had become friendship and friendship had become something far deeper. Mary's guilt tendrilled through her veins like kudzu. If she could have stopped loving the pup, she would have, but the truth was, the pup needed her. And Mary had never been able to turn her back on someone in need. Together, Mary knew, she and the pup could accomplish great things.

Still, her love for the pup ate at her. Every embrace, every laugh they shared, was stolen from Ryska. Somehow she had to find a way to give them back. To atone for her disloyalty.

She'd woken one morning with hope back at her throat and the plan, full-grown, in her mind. She wasn't being disloyal to Ryska after all. She was saving Ryska. And her seal pup, who had such beautiful aspirations, was part of that salvation.

Or so she'd believed. Now that, too, was sand in her hand.

Mary wondered if the pup would know, when she returned to the cabin, that their dream had died a hard death. Mary thought so. How could the pup fail to see it in her eyes? All they would have left now was each other.

She wasn't giving up on Ryska, Mary told herself, with all the grit she could muster. She just needed to rest. A little respite. Then she and the pup would try again. They would formulate a new plan, carve out a new path for Ryska to walk home on. She wasn't giving up. She would never give up.

But, Mother of God, she needed to rest.

She couldn't get rid of the realtor fast enough the next morning. Those people were so convinced of their own charm. *I'm a people person,* Mary imagined the woman blathering on to her friends. *It's all about relationships. It's all about rapport.*

Save me from these yammering magpies and their fascination with themselves, Mary thought drily. All she wanted to do was sign the contract, plant the sign, and drive away. But the woman thought she had to win Mary over first. Mary clung to the dregs of her patience and let the woman show her teeth and flap her tongue till she finally wore herself out.

She'd be back to finish packing in a few days. Now, all she wanted to do was reach the silence of the wilderness and wrap the seal pup in her arms and pretend that she had one more step left in her. One step. One step at a time, and eventually, she would reach the light again.

Mary watched the outside temperature gauge rising as she drove. Autumns in Alaska were shockingly brief. One day the mountains were awash in colors and bursting with berries, the next the trees were bare-armed and the ground washed with deathly pallor. The leaves had long since fallen, and there would be no more warm days until late spring. Today, though, despite looming clouds to the east, temperatures were creeping well above freezing. Driving would be that much easier if she didn't have to worry about ice on the roads. Likely it would refreeze before she headed back to Juneau, but that was only to be expected. Mary was long accustomed to the treachery of Alaskan roads.

As she drove, eyes peeled for any moose that might be gathering on the blacktop, Mary indulged herself, imagining what it would be like to spend the long dark winter months tucked away in the quiet refuge of the cabin. Before she came back for good, she thought, she'd pick up some jigsaw puzzles and new board games. Several new reams of wool. She should go Christmas shopping, too, so there'd be no need to go back to town for a while.

Her natural pragmatism nagged at her. She'd have to maintain some sort of foothold in regular society, at least until her house was sold. It wasn't as if the cabin had Wi-Fi or satellite communication, nor did she intend to install them. And given that winter wasn't exactly the hot selling season for real estate in Alaska, she wouldn't be able to make her retreat complete until the spring, at least. But next winter…next winter would be lovely. She sighed, sipping hot tea from her tumbler as she drove one-handed. For now, she would daydream and plan.

When she arrived at the cabin, the pup was carrying in an armful of wood. Eventually Mary supposed it wouldn't hurt her heart anymore to see how the pup limped. In so many ways, the uneven gait was part of the pup's new beauty, one that wasn't marred with paint and ornament and affectation. Her loveliness now was all earned rather than put on. The long dark hair, grown out past her shoulders again, lacked its former sheen but was dressed by the wind. Her eyes, which had sometimes gleamed with that curious mixture of avarice and joy peculiar to politicians, now layered shadows upon shadows, dark doors opening onto darker rooms full of mysteries she carried like talismans. Her creamy brown skin shone like a child's instead of a woman groomed for photo and film.

The pup smiled and waved but continued into the cabin through the back door as Mary shut off the ATV and unlocked the front, carrying in her bags of goodies. The seal pup knelt by the wood stove, adding a couple of logs and stacking the rest on the bricks. As Mary entered, the pup rose to wrap her in a warm embrace.

The seal pup sensed her despair, Mary was sure of it. There was something different in this hug. Strength emanated from the pup's arms, strength and comfort and almost desperation. The tears that had abandoned Mary in Juneau welled in her eyes now, and she scrubbed fiercely at her eyes as she pulled back. Serenity gleamed in the pup's eyes as she gently stroked Mary's iron-gray hair.

Mary took three trips back and forth to the car on the ATV. She'd brought extra clothes and more food than usual, in preparation for the coming months when she'd be spending much more time out here. The pup's eyes widened as Mary brought in bag after bag, folding and sorting her belongings into the bottom drawer of the little dresser and creating a bookshelf of sorts out of cardboard boxes to organize toiletries and craft supplies.

But Mary saved the best for last. As always, the pup watched eagerly to see what new delights Mary had brought, scurrying to place foodstuffs in just their right places. Mary didn't remember the pup being that organized in Juneau—if anything, she'd been a bit scattered—but here in the cabin, she reveled in precision. Foods were organized by type and then alphabetically—except for what she'd canned herself, which were gloriously ordered by color. The tiny kitchen with its open pantry shelves was a thing of beauty, Mary acknowledged. Much like the carefully curated flower garden, though its blooms were a briefer pleasure.

Mary waited till the pup's eyes had returned to her, her hands down at the bottom of her backpack. Drawing out the suspense, she slowly withdrew her last prize: the two tattered picture books she'd had to take from the pup, so long ago.

A long sigh shuddered from the pup's open mouth. Moving by increments, her outstretched hands trembling, the pup crept forward. With a shaky smile, Mary placed the books in the pup's hands. Keening softly, the pup sank to the floor, stroking the covers with reverent hands for a long time before she even turned a page. Tears glistened on her cheeks, but the pup dashed them away before they could mar the precious pages.

She stayed like that, cross-legged on the floor and thoroughly engaged in her stories while Mary cooked supper and boiled water for tea. The bleak and bitter darkness that had held Mary in its grasp since the election eased away, its edges lit by color like morning fog shot through with sunlight as it flees the night. Surely she could build some peace here.

Guilt crept back in on kitten-toes, but for once Mary chased it out. Her Ryska wouldn't begrudge her a few weeks or months of quiet, after all these many years of fighting. It wasn't as if she was abandoning the search. Regrouping, that was all. Creating a new life with her seal pup wasn't the same as carrying on in the regular world as if Ryska had never been there, had never been lost. That would have been unbearable. But out here, with the trees and the water and the wind, and the pup who might have been a sister to Ryska, Mary imagined that Ryska could feel her presence. That her little rabbit knew her mother longed after her, always, and that every kindness given to the pup was counted a kindness for her rabbit's sake.

Strange, Mary mused, that here of all places, where she'd never stood at the same time as Ryska, she felt closer to her than anywhere else. Perhaps it was just on account of all those weekends she'd spent scouring these woods, praying to find Ryska lost or injured or disoriented. Perhaps it was because here, she could serve the seal pup in all the ways she prayed someone, somewhere, was serving Ryska. Maybe it was just because for the first time in such a long, long time, she felt like a mother again.

She poured the pup a cup of tea and set it on the floor, where the pup remained raptly intent on her books, her fingers tracing every letter as if it were Braille. Dinner would be bacon and jalapeño corn chowder, with lofty cheese biscuits and lots of butter. Mary had never been a fully domesticated mother. Single working parents served a lot of preservatives and pizza, but cooking for the pup soothed something in her soul even as she regretted not having time to cook more often for Ryska. This had actually been one of Ryska's favorite meals. Mary tried to cook real food at least three or four times a week, but certain times of the year that just hadn't been possible. And unlike nearly every other Alaskan child Mary knew, Ryska had despised salmon. The only seafood she liked were shrimp and halibut and scallops. This chowder had been one of her favorite dishes.

The next two weeks were paradise. Every night she read to the seal pup from her picture books. In the mornings, they slept late, huddled under the covers as the fire sputtered into silence, and the sun sleepily trudged just over the horizon and stayed there. In the afternoons, Mary chopped and stacked wood. Every evening she cooked dinner, making a list as she went of what supplies she should bring back next time, what recipes she thought the pup would like best. She took a sip of vodka now and then, just for maintenance, but the thirst didn't claw at her like it had before.

The unseasonably warm temperatures held, often creeping nearly to fifty degrees, so after she'd chopped wood and had a cup of tea, she and the seal pup often went on walks under the pastel autumn skies. No flowers left to pick for weeks now, but they gathered branches and grasses and wove wreaths dotted with pinecones. They banged nails into the exterior of the cabin and festooned it with wreaths everywhere. Every now and then, Mary thought the shadows in the seal pup's eyes lifted. The light that shone through warmed places she'd thought irrevocably frozen.

But Mary had to go back. She needed to do more packing, sell off as much furniture and belongings as she could, wrap up her affairs. See how the house sale was going. She needed to make herself enter Ryska's room and empty it out.

She cupped the seal pup's thin cheek in her palm and pressed a kiss to her forehead. Perhaps the pup could wear some of Ryska's old clothes. No, that was silly. They were ancient. Probably rotten. She pulled the pup's forehead against her own and closed her eyes. The pup grasped both her forearms in her slender-fingered hands.

When finally, reluctantly, she pulled back, Mary was startled by the expression in the pup's somber gaze. That was no seal pup.

That was Noni.

Mary shook her head, blinked hard.

The seal pup gazed back at her, liquid eyes warm with affection, trust, and love.

She was just distraught to be leaving the pup after such a wonderful respite. Soon enough, she told herself, she would be back. One week at most; no more. This was her home. This was where she belonged. This was her daughter. Daughter of her heart.

But as the ATV roared away, something deep in Mary's spirit wailed. Silently she pleaded with the one-eyed Star-People to keep watch over her pup while she was away. Keep her safe.

AFTER THE ELECTION
Noni Begay

She left Rabbit on the windowsill, looking out toward the woods where the bones lay buried.

Beaver Woman took her left hand. Ryska took her right. Even through the three pairs of socks she'd pulled on as makeshift mittens, Noni felt their combined warmth and strength emanating up her arms. The last rumble of the ATV engine scarcely died out before they set out.

Solid ground met her feet, held fast in a hard frost. Bleak winter sun sparkled through droplets of ice clinging to the pushki stalks. Before her, Noni saw a ribbon of emerald green stretching away, over the sleeping earth.

Noni was wide awake.

Together, they walked out of the woods.

Missing Senator Found Alive

Juneau, **AK** – Missing Senator-Elect Noni Begay, who vanished without a trace immediately following her election more than six years ago, has been found alive, according to a spokesperson from the Alaska Fish and Game Division. Spokesperson Jan Neeley stated that Begay had already escaped on her own when she encountered game wardens in the area on an unrelated poaching investigation. Though the State Troopers have yet to issue an official statement, Begay's former campaign manager and the recent senatorial candidate, Mary Nelson, who lost to Bob Rinehart, has been booked into jail on charges of aggravated kidnapping, first-degree assault, and false imprisonment, among other charges. The Begay family released this statement: "We are overwhelmingly grateful that our daughter has been found alive. We never gave up hope that she would return home. We ask that everyone respect our family's privacy and give Noni time to heal and recover." Updates will be posted online when they become available.

Missing Native Woman Found Dead

Juneau, AK – In a bizarre turn of events, kidnapped Senator-Elect Noni Begay, who was just found alive after having escaped her captor, has led authorities to the decomposed body of another missing native woman, positively identified as Ryska Nelson. Ryska Nelson was the daughter of Begay's own captor and former campaign manager, Mary Nelson. However, the two cases are considered to be only peripherally related. According to Begay, Nelson was motivated to kidnap her in an effort to bring national attention to the issue of Missing and Murdered Indigenous Women and Girls (MMIWG) in hopes of finding her own daughter, who had gone missing ten years prior to Begay's abduction. Tragically, Nelson had conducted multiple searches of her own in the very area where Ryska's body was found. Police have not yet named a suspect, but Ryska Nelson's former boyfriend Liam Reynolds is sought for questioning. Reynolds' last known location was in Montana, but he has been known to frequently return to Alaska for work on the oil rigs. Anyone with information regarding his whereabouts, or any information regarding the case of Ryska Nelson, is asked to contact the Alaska State Troopers or the FBI.

Mary Nelson Sentenced To Prison

Juneau, AK - Former senatorial candidate Mary Nelson, who lost last year's election in a hotly contested race and pled guilty last month to multiple charges related to the kidnapping of former Senator-Elect Noni Begay, was sentenced Monday to fourteen years in prison. In an unexpected turn of events, the victim testified on behalf of the accused, pleading with the court to show mercy. Judge Rachel Valynski stated that while she was deeply moved by Begay's testimony, she could not consider it justice unless Nelson served at least as many years in prison as Begay had suffered imprisonment in the remote wilderness cabin where she was held for nearly seven years. Valynski then sentenced Nelson to twice that amount of time, since prison overcrowding likely guarantees she will only serve half her term. The prison sentence will be followed by a further twenty year suspended sentence, during which time Nelson will be supervised.

Related story: Still No Charges In Case Of Murdered Native Woman Ryska Nelson

THE END OF THINGS
Mary Nelson

Like curling bark, caught out of the fire by a gust of wind, brittle newsprint slipped out of Mary's fingers and danced to the concrete floor. Her fingers, dried and calloused, struggled to chase the shredded pages. She blinked in the dim half-light that was the nearest thing to night in this existence bound by steel and solitude.

The solitude was her own creation, of course. In reality, privacy and independence were the first of the human dignities stripped from a prisoner. Shunted door to door, cell to common room to cell, in masses like cattle trained to respond to a harsh bark, a whistle, or a bell, inmates lost most resemblance to sentient creatures and seemed instead led entirely by instinct and reflex. Showering, shitting, changing clothes, weeping, masturbating, eating, sleeping, all became performance arts in which no one had any real interest but from which no one looked away, either. Whatever extremities of reason or emotion Mary suffered, she suffered it in public, always in public, because there is no private in prison. Her sheets, her papers, her person were all subject to search at any time, and the sensation of strange hands brushing over her uniform and strange voices ordering her to bend and spread became unremarkable.

These unrelenting incursions, casual or calculated, couldn't reach Mary. Sometimes the other women protested their treatment, rebelled against the hands and the voices and the handcuffs, but Mary hardly even heard their complaints. Her own compliance was without generosity, a simple refusal to engage even to the point of resistance. The guards quickly learned she was no target for their infrequent reprisals against the gambling or gang violence or bootlegging that were the normal order of society inside; she'd have had to make a friend or an enemy first, and Mary was nothing more than a ghost inside these walls. Initially a few inmates had tried either consolation or taunting to reach the older woman, whose crime and grief were both sensational enough to merit favor, but they had quickly given up.

Even in her prosecution, she had declined to speak beyond insisting that she would plead guilty. She'd offered no explanation, no defense, uttered no pleas for mercy. When her frustrated attorney insisted on a psychological evaluation, arguing that she was not able to assist in her own defense, a resigned psychologist had been forced to testify that Mary Nelson was fully capable and rational, just obstinate. She'd endured his questions and answered him just well enough, but that resolved, she simply declined to communicate with anyone else. Her own attorney's arguments for clemency had been perfunctory in the end, far less impassioned than the testimony of Noni Begay.

Mary's fingers shook as she gently scooped up the fallen scrap of paper, eyes blurring with the recollection of the seal pup's face as she had stood there in the witness stand. She had no longer sounded like a pup. Her voice had been that of a seal mother defending her own against an aggressive male, strident and fierce and strong. Mary, who had drifted further and further from her own body, had been yanked back into her bones. The song of the seal pup, raised against the roaring of the wind and the crashing of the surf, had banged and bellowed through Mary's veins, stirring her blood till she almost—*almost*—imagined that she too could speak the language of the seals and decipher the code of the strange melody.

She couldn't, of course. Walruses and seals don't speak the same tongue, even when they are friends. Still, as she raised her head in the cold courtroom and locked eyes with her seal pup, she felt peace pouring over her skin, a communion of creatures who needed no tongue.

That had been enough. Would have to be enough forever.

To find privacy, to find solitude in the prison walls had been no hardship. Let the other women become a herd, accept the fate of the domesticated. Mary felt no kinship with them. So they had wombs. So they had empty arms. So they had committed unspeakable acts and found themselves outcast. So they called each other sister, petted and stroked each other and pretended at comforts and solaces like friends instead of the opportunistic eaters they truly were. It was no matter to her. Their pretended intersections of commonality elicited no sympathies from Mary. She held her space sacred, less inclined to defend it than to disregard any advances against it. The other women were so many ants, occasionally to be avoided, occasionally to be stepped on, but never addressed or implored. They had as much reality to her as cottonwood fluff has to the ocean.

At first the women responded resentfully, shamed by her rebuffs and infuriated by their shame. How dare she reject them? Didn't she know who they were? Didn't she understand the importance of alliances in this bleak and brutal place? They quickly learned that while Mary might be quiet, she was far from meek. Her rigorous and rugged life outside had more than prepared her to deal with any junkie or meth-head who mistook her age for weakness. She only had to finish two fights she didn't start before everyone gave her a wide berth. Eventually acrimony simmered into respect, and Mary preferred it no better than she had the hate.

The guards or CO's or bosses or whatever the women wanted to call them were less divided in their reactions to their notorious inmate. She never made their job harder, after all, and wherever she walked or sat or slept, things tended to be calmer and quieter than anywhere else. When she'd first been arrested, it had taken some careful medical watches to detox her from the alcohol, but once she'd had it thoroughly washed from her system, she'd shown no inclination to reintroduce it. Bootleg stills were hidden everywhere in the cells and provided major currency for the inmates' sales of sex or commissary or gambling debts, but Mary had shown no interest in joining those ranks, not even just for personal consumption. She was a model prisoner, by all accounts. And who could not look with compassion on the old Native woman with her grief cut like rivers in her face?

That compassion, unsought and unregistered, had salvaged these bits of newsprint for her. All those years of resurrecting anniversaries had at last trained the coyotes just as she'd once wished. This November, the first anniversary of Noni Begay's disappearance since her abductor had been sentenced, the newspapers and television media had delightedly unearthed the story and splayed out its bones one more time. Striding along on her regular tireless circuits of the dayroom, its path left unobstructed for her by the other women's caution, she'd seen the words scrolling along the bottom of the television screens. As if she'd needed the reminder. And what purpose did it serve now? Once she'd spent weeks looking forward to the date, hoping that this year would be the year that brought forward some new witness, some new lead, this year would be the year she brought her Ryska home. She'd harassed every media person she knew, from national broadcasters to local podcasters, bullying them into giving her even a few scant seconds of airtime. Now that it could do no good at all, everyone wanted to write a feature, create a biopic, film some sensational special to glut the public's hunger for horror.

Mary wondered how many other girls had gone missing since she'd arrived here in this huge, breathing coffin where she would be buried. How many other Natives had been murdered and discarded as refuse without so much as a one-line mention in the papers? How many mothers had sent disregarded emails to the press, had called the FBI, had organized scattered search parties, had stood on rainy steps with tattered signs decked in running ink? How many names were wailed on the wind, returning empty? Meanwhile, her seal pup and her rabbit had become icons, pop-culture props emblazoned on t-shirts and posterboards, their names recited like a rosary that would bring people closer to God for having re-membered them. But what of all the other names? Unconsciously, Mary's hand reached for her cross, finding the empty space between her breasts where it had hung.

In a rare fury, Mary charged around the dayroom tables, scooping up ev-ery newspaper she could find. Unaccustomed to her rage but well-aware of her strength, the other women pushed themselves back out of her way, offering no resistance to her sudden thievery. Ryska and Noni's faces had been emblazoned on the front page. Mary had ripped off each sheet and torn them into shreds that heaped on the dirty concrete before stuffing the rest of the papers in the com-munal trash bin.

Two acts of kindness, which were more common inside than Mary would have known, intruded here. Another older woman, who'd understood at least some fraction of Mary's outburst, had painfully lowered herself to the hard floor and begun salvaging the torn paper. Two bone-thin junkies, eager for some hu-manity they could cling to, joined her. The three of them spread out the tattered remains of four newspaper pages on a dayroom table and matched up the pieces until they had the complete story in puzzle, discarding all the redundancies. They took their fractured treasure to the CO on duty and made their request.

Which won the second act of kindness. Whether moved by sympathy for an inmate who rarely gave a day's trouble, or touched by the simple decency of the three women before her, the guard agreed to save the pieces, carefully plac-ing them in a manila envelope labeled *Nelson*. Late that night, while most of the women slept, the guard turned her key in Mary's cell door. Mary's cellmate, whose name she never learned, snored uninterrupted in the bottom bunk. Mary, who maybe never slept at all, sat up, her dark eyes bright and alert as she met the guard's steady gaze.

The guard simply lifted the envelope in Mary's direction, laid it on the steel desk, and exited the cell. The bunkmate moaned softly and rolled over at the reverberating clang. Mary jumped softly down to the floor, her knees hardly protesting. She padded to the desk in her sock feet, hardly registering the cold seeping through the thin material. She shook out the contents of the envelope, choking back a sob as she recognized them.

Grief loves rage, prefers it above all other companions. Anger is the only thing with teeth sharp enough to distract grief from its own gaping wound. But anger is a cat, fickle and unreliable, prone to bursts of wild speed followed by unshaken somnolence. It wears itself out too quickly to provide true ease to the heart. Mary's fury had blown itself out as swiftly as it had blown in, leaving her hollow and dry.

Ryska's blurred face, torn by Mary's own hands, stared up at her, the half-smile an expression of forever suspended hope and joy. This new grief, which had too quickly become old and familiar and sometimes even latent, swamped her flesh, gutting her like a fish drowning in the air. She keened, clutching at her belly, a long, terrifying wail whose unending sorrow struck horror in the hearts of all who heard it. Her bunkmate, yanked out of sleep, started instinctively forward to comfort her, but wisely shrank back before she could reach the mourner and retreated instead to the interior of her blankets.

In the gloom of the sleeping pod, the hardened old guard paused on her rounds, tears starting to her eyes at the awful sound.

More awful than the wail were the garbled sounds that followed, a jumble of remorses and avowals and pitiful pet names. To the bunkmate huddled on the bed, it was as if a grievously wounded animal, lying by the freshly slain carcass of its young, had suddenly been given a human voice. Frightening and dreadful and utterly forlorn, the sounds echoed in the small room until the bunkmate sobbed helplessly in unwilling commiseration with her erstwhile sister.

Horror compounded horror as every detail of her little rabbit's discovery rushed back over Mary. She had known, hadn't she, known from the beginning, but somehow that rotten, rancid fungus hope had cast its spores in her heart and overgrown it. How many times had she searched that property, certain that the answers to her little rabbit's fate lay there? She'd yelled herself hoarse in the early days, hoping against hope that Ryska was hurt, lost, tied up, somehow unable to rescue herself but still alive. What if she had been? What if she'd heard her mother's voice? What if she hadn't been killed right away but had suffered and struggled, in pain and fear, all alone in the cold and the dark and the wet?

Mary imagined her little rabbit starting, straining, at the sound of her mother's voice, longing for salvation, for succor, only to sink into abject despair as the calls faded and finally fell into silence. Tormenting herself with that possibility had become the closest thing Mary had to comfort. She wanted to hurt, she wanted to bleed, she wanted to spill out her intestines and squeeze them in her fists until the anguish blotted out all conscious thought. Mary could never take up her baby's pain. She'd lost the capacity for joy, for beauty; she could only find her daughter now in agonies, and finding Ryska, holding Ryska, even if only in death, was all she knew how to do.

Even when all chance of an answering call had been lost, Mary had searched the woods with a shotgun on her back and a long wooden stick in her hand, looking for any sign of scavengers and pushing aside the bounding ferns and hanging mosses. She hadn't acknowledged then, even to herself, that she was hunting for a body. She'd told herself only that she was looking for Ryska. Somehow she'd missed her, somehow her mother's instinct had failed her. Her daughter had lain there under a pathetically, disrespectfully shallow layer of loam, rotting, decaying, eaten by bugs and gnawed at by rodents, while her mother had raised a seal pup only a few hundred yards away. How could she not have found her? Did she not love her enough? Had she shrunk back in horror from her own efforts, had she somehow instinctively avoided a truth that, like her daughter, was already long dead and unalterable?

Mary clutched at her belly and rocked back and forth on the concrete, her long grey hair flowing unbound down her broad back. How could she live with this pain? Why wouldn't her wretched heart just stop beating? Her lungs stop their tiresome seizing and relenting?

When she'd first arrived, she hadn't eaten, thinking that her system would abandon its paltry efforts at sustaining itself and give up. She'd quickly learned that refusing food took more effort than eating it, though, and she had no energy for extra efforts. So she consumed enough to pass without notice, and more and more day by day her body insisted on propelling itself forward.

Tonight, though, the pain came on fresh, as though brand new. Seeing Ryska's name in print, hearing it on the lips of strangers who never loved her, seemed a final affront to a woman-child who had suffered enough affront already. After all these years of fighting to make her daughter famous so that she could bring her safely home, Mary couldn't bear that Ryska had become a household name only in death. The coyotes and the cormorants recounted their poor facts as if they told a story: junkie, single-parent home, abusive boyfriend and dealer, Native, "at-risk," but Ryska had been more than all that—and less, too.

She'd been a terrible fisherwoman and a worse hunter. She'd stand in the surf and cast her line, but she paid more attention to sea stars and otters than to her pole. At least she had the stomach to gut and clean her catch on the rare occasion when she made one, but she was too tender-hearted to even draw a bead on a hunt. At first Mary had tried to take her along, sure that the girl would learn the ways with time, but no talk of honor and respect and the spirits could persuade her to take a life. That had never stopped her from eating the bounty with gusto, though, once it was fully stripped of its fur and feathers. So Mary had acquiesced and allowed her daughter to sit out the annual hunts.

Ryska'd been equally tender-hearted toward people, especially the ones Mary tended to dismiss. She'd argued against her mother's cynical views, insisting they roll down the window when a bum stood at the intersection, handing out her own lunch or whatever change she had in her pocket. She would sit for hours on the riverbank, and her cell phone camera had been crammed with photos of wildflowers and baby moose instead of selfies.

She'd been a hunter in her own way, Mary reflected, a hunter of the good and the beautiful. She saw it even where it wasn't, or at least where Mary was sure it wasn't. In the junkie friends who offered her no aid when her boyfriend used her a punching bag, in her dealer boyfriend, in the trashy little trailer that she'd decked out with thrift store curtains and salvage yard flower vases she painted herself. But her little rabbit had been flawed, broken, and not all her cracks could be filled with gold. Some of them were filled with heroin and meth, and bit by bit the ceramic flaked away.

Oh, Ryska, Ryska, Ryska. My baby girl. My broken, broken girl. I'm so sorry.

Mary gasped, long shuddering breaths that felt as though they could never bring her enough air. Her face damp but her eyes dry and red, she brushed her hair behind her ears and blinked hard to clear her vision, forcing her eyes to focus. People said she would feel better if she just cried it out, but it wasn't true. She felt worse, emptier and emptier, as if her spirit were eternally being drawn further and further away from her heart. Where spirit had been, pain remained, sloshing and splashing in a well that only grew deeper every night. One day her heart would be completely dried out, cured, hard as a fruit stone and incapable of one more beat. She yearned for that day.

But this was not that day.

Painstakingly, Mary reached for the fallen newsprint and began sorting them out on the floor. A moan escaped her lips as she ordered Ryska's beautiful face. Her hand trembled over the shattered image, fingers outstretched as if she could stroke those soft brown cheeks one more time, feel the whisper of Ryska's long minky lashes falling downward. Never again. All her life was an accounting of nevers.

Mary pushed herself off the floor and retrieved her supplies: her cup of water, her toothpaste, and a few pieces of blank white paper. A little toothpaste and water made an excellent glue of sorts. She pasted the blank pages together to form a large enough square on which to center her reconstituted news article, and with slow, precise movements, pasted each puzzle piece into its construct on the paper.

Something in the regular and exact work soothed her, lulling her into a near-trance. Grief retreated into sadness, into a familiar and bearable current that coursed through her body without interrupting every other function. Her bunkmate, worn out with her own crying, had fallen back asleep, and her rumbling snores offered a hypnotic rhythm to Mary's undertaking.

She wondered what the seal pup was doing now. If she had learned to fish on her own. Mary knew she'd been too protective in the end. Even pups needed to break out into open water on their own. For so long she'd thought that she and the pup had the same goals, the same dreams. And maybe they had. But even after all her training, all her devotion, the pup had clung to some innate sense of self, some definition of her existence that to this day remained utterly foreign to Mary. The pup had only been a fosterling, after all. Maybe it was inevitable that they should be parted in the end. Even though they shared the sea, a walrus and a seal did not move the same among the currents. It would have to be enough that they loved each other. Maybe love was all there was. Maybe no one understood anyone. Maybe every spirit cried out to the stars in a singular song that no other spirit ever comprehended. Still some melodies did cling to each other. Mary did not understand the aurora's song either, but her heart thrilled to watch it playing on the winter sky.

She hoped the pup had found safe waters.

Placing the last scrap of newsprint in place, she traced the outline of the story with a careful finger. Some words were missing, some lines lost. More than any coyote could identify. Leaning forward over her crossed legs, she blew a gentle breath across the page. Her tongue felt unwieldy as she spoke aloud.

"I will say your name, my little rabbit. I will say your name."

Mary Nelson's bunkmate slept restlessly, her dreams punctuated by the repetition of a single word that intruded in every scene: *Ryska, Ryska, Ryska*. When she blearily emerged from her blankets to stumble out into the dayroom for breakfast, though, the cell had fallen silent. Mary Nelson lay outstretched on the hard floor, curtained iron falling over her face, her hand resting on the restored news article beside her head. Her bunkmate started to step over her legs, then paused, something in the stillness stiffening her spine.

"Guard! Guard!"

Later they would say it was a catastrophic stroke, but as the seal pup scattered her ashes over the depressed hollow in the wood where Ryska's bones had lain so long, she knew better. Some wounds, however long ago delivered, are always mortal.

"I will say your name," said Noni Begay. "I will say your name, Mary Nelson."

Author's Note

Much of this book's scaffolding is experimental. One of the supports which readers may or may not notice is that only women have a voice in this story, even though there are several men who play pivotal roles.

The mythological *K't-talqani, K'etetaalkkaanee*, or the Beaver Man, a heroic shapeshifter known in indigenous Alaskan lore as the Wanderer, becomes Beaver Woman as Noni Begay identifies herself with him. The tales of "The Moon and His Wife" and "The Girl Who Searched for Her Lover" are also reinterpreted by the characters of this book in ways that fit their own longings for hope and understanding. Every story is transformed in the mouth of a new storyteller. This is not intended to be in any way disrespectful to the original tales, but only a testament to their power and transcendental timelessness.

Despite the fact that Alaska is by far the least densely populated of all US states, with a population of much fewer than one million people in an area more than double the size of Texas, it has the fourth highest incidence of missing and murdered indigenous women and girls, and Anchorage holds the position of third highest city in that regard, according to a 2018 report by the Urban Indian Health Institute. But this is not an Alaska problem. It is a North American problem. Murder is the third leading cause of death for Native women, who are, according to 2016 CDC statistics, ten times more likely to die by homicide than all other ethnicities. This has to change. The police and the politicians can't fix this. Won't fix this. But we can. And we must.

Acknowledgements

This book was written during the six years I lived in Alaska. Although I was aware of the crisis of missing and murdered indigenous women and girls before that, once I shared the earth and sea there with so many who walked only in spirit, I became consumed by their stories. From the bottom of my heart, I thank every person who has shared a piece of themselves with me. Every stranger, friend, acquaintance, hitchhiker, hater, and enemy. Most especially I would like to thank the many Native storytellers, archivists, artists, and poets who continue to chronicle and tell the stories old and new. The mothers, fathers, sisters, brothers, and friends who stand and march and say the names of the lost until their throats are hoarse.

About the Author

Cassondra Windwalker earned a BA of Letters from the University of Oklahoma. Born and raised on the red clay, she's wandered the sticky corn fields of the Midwest, the frozen seas of the Wild North, and frequently rests her wings where orange skies meet purple mountains. She's the author of nine novels and three works of poetry who does her best to keep fed a menagerie of stray critters, cryptids, marooned kelpies, and lost specters. She enjoys interacting with readers, writers, and generally decent humans on social media.

Past publications include *What Hides in the Cupboards, Love Like a Cephalopod, Hold My Place,* and many more. Her next release, *The Gardener's Wife's Mistress*, is expected in 2026.

Find her on X @WindwalkerWrite, on Instagram @cassondrawindwalker, and on Facebook and YouTube @CassondraWindwalkerWrites.

(Photo by the author)

Also Available from Polymath Press

Case Files of the Rocky Mountain Paranormal Research Society Volumes 1 & 2 by Robert Lewis & Bryan Bonner

For over a quarter of a century, the Rocky Mountain Paranormal Research Society has investigated ghosts, aliens, cryptids, and all manner of bizarre claims and happenings in Colorado and beyond. Combining historic and scientific research with a love of the weird and scary, they've researched and documented some of the best paranormal stories in the world. Now, Colorado's first and only forensic paranormal investigation team is proud to present the first two volumes of their collected case files.

Within these pages, you'll learn not only the ghostly and paranormal stories, but the histories of the allegedly haunted locations and the methods Rocky Mountain Paranormal uses to get to the bottom of some of the world's strangest phenomena.

And don't miss the exciting third volume, expected in Fall of 2025!